If someone had thought to include a photo in the pathetically thin file, Theo would not have been thinking boring or average. The woman sitting on the forest floor glaring up at him with eyes so searingly shockingly blue was not average or boring.

"What are you doing here anyway?"

Her accusing words brought his attention back to the moment, and the figure sitting at his feet.

"Did I need to ask permission?"

His mockery pushed color into her pale cheeks.

"We had no idea you were coming. A bit of warning might have been nice." It sounded petulant and she felt stupid, especially as she was not exactly operating from a position of authority.

"Just checking you haven't stolen the silver."

As his lazy mockery touched a nerve and burnt like acid, her chin went up. "Very funny." Then the very real mortifying possibility he wasn't joking hit her.

"Half of it is mine," she countered, observing from the flare of his nostrils that he hadn't liked that. Well good, she was glad!

Kim Lawrence lives on a farm in Anglesey with her university-lecturer husband, assorted pets who arrived as strays and never left, and sometimes one or both of her boomerang sons. When she's not writing, she loves to be outdoors gardening or walking on one of the beaches for which the island is famous—along with being the place where Prince William and Catherine made their first home!

Books by Kim Lawrence

Harlequin Presents

Claimed by Her Greek Boss

A Ring from a Billionaire

Waking Up in His Royal Bed
The Italian's Bride on Paper

Jet-Set Billionaires

Innocent in the Sicilian's Palazzo

The Secret Twin Sisters

The Prince's Forbidden Cinderella
Her Forbidden Awakening in Greece

Visit the Author Profile page
at Harlequin.com for more titles.

Kim Lawrence

AWAKENED IN HER ENEMY'S PALAZZO

Recycling programs for this product may not exist in your area.

ISBN-13: 978-1-335-59235-4

Awakened in Her Enemy's Palazzo

Harlequin Enterprises ULC
22 Adelaide St. West, 41st Floor
Toronto, Ontario M5H 4E3, Canada
www.Harlequin.com

Printed in U.S.A.

AWAKENED IN HER ENEMY'S PALAZZO

For Dan, thanks for stepping in last minute!

CHAPTER ONE

THEO STOOD BY the glass wall, hands thrust deep into his pockets, presenting a perfect patrician profile to the four other men in the boardroom. Theo thought very little, if at all, about his profile. He had his faults, as he would be the first to acknowledge—though not apologise for—but vanity was not one of them, despite the fact that even his most severe critics agreed he had plenty to be vain about.

Being six feet four, and blessed with an impressively athletic physique that impeccable tailoring did nothing to disguise, ensured that Theo was an attention-grabbing figure in any setting. Combined with his physical presence he possessed razor-sharp instincts and a reputation for forensic attention to detail that meant no one came into any meeting where he was present unprepared.

Today, his normal ability to focus on detail was not functioning at full capacity. He wasn't absorbing more than one word in three—a circumstance which was obvious to those around him. But although a few subtly raised eyebrows and loaded glances were exchanged between the nervous-looking suited figures delivering expensive advice to him, none of them mentioned the fact that their target audience appeared to be supremely uninterested in it.

The current speaker paused, losing his thread as he found himself no longer speaking to a pair of broad shoulders but instead to a pair of jet-black eyes, obsidian-dark and inscrutable. He straightened up in his seat, exhaling slightly as the tall Italian, hands thrust deep in the pockets of his tailored suit trousers, turned back to his appraisal of the panoramic view, his expression set in a scowl of irritation.

The irritation was aimed at himself. Theo hated the fact that his thoughts were all over the place. Although that was not strictly true. He knew exactly where they were—in Tuscany.

An image of the palazzo where he had grown up floated into his head and he pushed it away—but not before he had seen himself as a child, laying flowers on his mother's grave, his tears falling onto the dry, dusty ground as he swore to hate his father for ever.

He pressed his fingertips to his temple, where a blue vein beat, as he stared out, seeing for the first time the rain that had been falling for the last half-hour.

Was it raining in Tuscany as Salvatore was being laid to rest in the family crypt beside his late wife? Or was the sun shining as the great and the good of Italian society, and also the not so good, dressed in designer black listened to the priest lie about what a good man his father had been?

He'd thought that once too. He had worshipped the man. And then he had discovered the truth. He'd been thirteen years old at the time, still in his black funeral suit, hiding in a cupboard to cry the tears he had held in during his mother's funeral because his mother had not liked him to cry. It had made her unhappy.

'Why are you not going to your father's funeral?' Cleo had asked as he'd left her apartment that morning.

The scantily clad luscious redhead had been lazily curious, and not judgemental or particularly surprised when he had not responded to her question while she carefully reapplied her red lipstick.

That was what made Cleo a perfect companion for him. Along with her voracious sexual appetite, she was fine with his silences and didn't make any demands.

Hadn't made demands, he silently corrected in his head.

He had reached the door when that situation had changed—when she had voiced the fatal words that had brought him back into the room.

'So, where do we go from here, darling?'

His response had been short and to the point. Other people equated honesty with cruelty, but not Theo. He believed the truth was just the truth; it was not emotive, just fact.

'Nowhere,' he'd told her.

It had ended neatly, the way he liked things—neat, simple and uncomplicated by messy emotions. It was a pity… Cleo was beautiful, desirable, and until *that* question had been exactly the sort of female he was attracted to. A talented, successful woman, as single-minded and as ambitious as he was, with a life that was separate from his. It had been a positive that they did not share friends or opinions. She was not interested in going anywhere with him outside the bedroom or the occasional photo opportunity public event.

There had been a time when he had been concerned that some sort of chemistry with a woman might at some point cause him to over-rule his decision that marriage was not for him.

His concern had been misplaced.

If it had been going to happen, he reasoned, it

would have done so by now. He had had plenty of *chemistry* with women, but none of it had made him lose his mind enough to forget that nothing lasted for ever—certainly not sexual attraction. And what else kept two people together? Except perhaps laziness and a lack of options.

To Theo's way of thinking there were two sorts of marriage: those that ended in messy divorce and those that continued in lies.

The former was, to his mind—while messy and expensive—infinitely preferable. But then he had had a front row seat for the latter. To the world, his parents' marriage had been perfect—but it had been an act they had perpetuated to disguise their mutual misery.

A shaft of sunlight had appeared through the clouds when he finally turned back to the room full of lawyers. He scanned them, the seemingly relaxed stance of his tall, rangy frame in contrast to the expectant tension emanating from the group.

'I want to sell.'

His simple words were greeted by a stunned silence and collective dropped jaws.

'Sell...?' one of the lawyers queried tentatively.

'Some land, you mean?' another interrupted, with a smile that suggested he was more in tune with the way the mind of a financial genius who had made his fortune in IT worked than his colleagues. 'That would be a financially sound move. The forest area—now, that is a piece of prime land with development opportunity written all over it. Obviously the eco lobby would have a fit, but I've never encountered a protection order that wasn't breakable, and the land on the southern boundary...'

His enthusiasm became genuine as he warmed to his theme.

Out of nowhere images of a cool green oasis...the dappled light, the silence, the tall swaying trees, an encounter with a deer or a wild boar...began to slide slowly through Theo's head.

His jaw clenched. He was determined to divest himself of any reminder of his past, and he prided himself on not being sentimental, but the idea of that green oasis being destroyed made nameless things tighten in his chest.

'You're talking about the forest on the northern slopes?' Theo pinned the man with an obsidian stare that made the guy shift uneasily in his seat and consult the blank screen of the tablet on the desk beside him.

'Northern—I think so. All mountain. Yes, not suitable for— But a holiday village would—'

Theo pushed away the image of denuded forest slopes and the sound of machinery. 'A nonstarter,' he said coolly. 'It is a protected area, and there are clauses in the deeds of the palazzo.'

'Of course. Palazzo della Stellato…such an evocative name.'

Theo responded to the man's exaggerated Italian pronunciation with a stony look.

'There are other sections that we have already had tentative enquiries about—from several developers who have made it known they would be interested. Let me see… The Wenger Group…'

As one man, all the legal team began to desperately scroll through their assorted devices.

'I have the details here. They approached your father last year, I believe, but he was never… Not a criticism, of course—he was old school, which was understandable, given the historic nature of the estate…'

'I'm not interested in history.' *Only escaping it.* 'And, no, I do not want to sell *some land.*'

The hand Theo ran across the dark surface of his dark hair suggested impatience that they couldn't keep up with him.

'The lot. The palazzo, the contents, the land—just get rid of it all. I want nothing.'

Just the portrait that had hung in his father's

study. Was it still there? he wondered. Had his
father kept it there to remind himself of his
guilt? Or had he rewritten the past to make it
easier to live with?

He could feel shocked eyes following him
as he left the room. Not that he cared, but all
the same he was glad he had bitten back the
unspoken rejoinder that had hovered on the tip
of his tongue.

*I want nothing that reminds me of that bas-
tard.*

It would have been sharing too much.

'Half?' Grace echoed. 'You mean half the
books?'

She glanced around the shelves of the library
they were sitting in. The lawyer was sitting in
the chair that Salvatore had sat in when she'd
read to him, and it made his absence more of
a stark reality than the funeral had.

'Oh, how kind. But I couldn't break up the
collection…it's far too valuable. One or two
books, maybe?'

'Miss Stewart, I don't think you quite understand…' the man said slowly. 'When I say
"half", I mean half of *everything*: the palazzo,
the estate, the money. It has been left jointly
to you both.'

Grace stared at him blankly for a moment,

and then laughed, although this wasn't funny. It was crazy. Which was most likely the way her laugh sounded too.

'He's left me—?' She had to have the wrong end of the stick. 'Why—no, that can't be right—go back and check. I think you'll find—' She half rose in her seat and collapsed weakly back again as her voice faded.

'Would you like a glass of water?'

The man whose neatly trimmed beard was flecked with white smiled kindly at her.

Grace shook her head, thinking she wouldn't have said no to a brandy. She held her clasped hands tight in her lap—not that it disguised the fact she was shaking. A few deep breaths and the volume of the buzzing in her head lessened, her temporary numbness melting away leaving shock and disbelief.

'You're not joking?' She almost immediately dismissed the idea. 'Sorry, no…no, of course not.'

Could lawyers joke?

Observation of her own immediate family—her brother was a member of that profession—suggested not, but then her other brother, the psychiatrist, never laughed at her jokes either. Nor her ecologist sister, whose TV series had just been sold to the States.

They were a gifted bunch, her family, and

they tried to be kind about Grace's deficiencies—the fact that Grace was not the most academically gifted of the Stewart clan. But she knew that her parents—her Oxford professor dad and historian mother, both acknowledged experts and bestselling authors in their fields—had been gutted when Grace had, to everyone's surprise, including her own, got the grades to secure a coveted Oxford place but had chosen instead to embark on a nursing degree.

'You are a very wealthy young woman.'

Grace dragged herself back to the very surreal present. 'Wealthy? I think you've made a mistake. I'm going home today. I have a week's holiday before I start my next—' She stopped and dragged in a gulping breath. 'That *can't* be right. Why would Salvatore leave me anything? I was only his nurse. I only knew him for a couple of months.'

What will people think or say?

Grace didn't voice the last thought out loud. There was no point asking a question when you already knew the answer.

They would think the worst possible thing. They would say there was no smoke without fire—just as they had the last time.

Her heart took a sickening lurch as those memories escaped the box she had locked them in, marked *I have moved on.*

It had been her second job for the nursing agency. A lovely, grateful family with whom she had been on the best of terms—until an extremely valuable necklace and a pile of cash had vanished.

It had been a nightmare.

Grace had been suspended, because the family who had days earlier been thanking her had suddenly been accusing her of being a thief. The truth had come out almost immediately, and she had been proved totally innocent, but the event had left scars.

This is not the same!

'This is… It feels surreal.'

'I can see this has been a shock…but a pleasant one?' The balding figure smiled benignly at her.

'No…yes… But I only knew him— This just isn't right. Can I give it back?'

'Give what back?'

'Everything… The staff can have it. Marta and…'

A hand was lifted to still halt her spill of anxious words. 'The staff have all been remembered very generously in the will, and tenants have been given lifetime tenure. Let me assure you that no one has been forgotten. I think you should take some time to get used to the idea, and then…'

'No. I was his nurse. I can't benefit financially from someone's death. People will think that I took advantage…'

'Not at all,' the lawyer soothed. But he was avoiding her eyes. Because obviously, human nature being what it was, some people would. He considered her for a moment and then, seeming to some to a decision, said, 'Look, if you do feel that way there is an option—though I advise you not to make any decisions yet…'

'What option?'

An hour later Grace walked into the massive kitchen, with its modern state-of-the-art equipment sitting comfortably on the original flagstone floor, among heavy beams and the original kitchen fireplace. No one would have described it as cosy, but it was the most informal room in the palazzo, which boasted too many bedrooms to count and was, unsurprisingly, designed on a palatial scale.

Marta, the housekeeper, wearing her usual crisp white blouse and tailored trousers, was sitting at the table, tapping into the spreadsheets on her laptop, as she sipped a cup of coffee. She looked up when Grace appeared.

'I know that computers are meant to make life easier, but honestly… This—' She stopped, the smile fading from her narrow face as she took in Grace's expression. 'Oh, my, you look pale.' The older woman tutted. 'It's been a hard few days. I wish you'd let me rearrange your flight for later in the week.'

Grace managed a distracted smile. When she'd arrived ten weeks ago the housekeeper, who had been very protective of her employer, had initially been suspicious of the English nurse suddenly living in the palazzo. She had openly questioned why an agency specialising in palliative end-of-life care had not sent an Italian-speaking nurse.

Grace herself had asked the same thing, and had been told that her patient, who was fluent in several languages, did not have a problem with her not speaking Italian.

'We have an army of nurses on rota here already. What are you? A miracle-worker?' Marta had asked scornfully. 'Are you going to make him live?'

Grace, who had heard grief talking before, had been gentle. 'I hope I'll be able to make him a little more comfortable.'

Marta's attitude had changed when she'd seen the difference the new regime of pain relief that Grace had introduced had made to her employer. And how she'd worked in conjunction with Salvatore's own physician, who was universally adored by the staff at the palazzo.

Grace had seen tears in her eyes the day she'd walked into the kitchen and found the previously bedbound Salvatore sitting at the table they were seated at now.

'He was just surviving,' Marta had said in the emotional aftermath of the funeral. 'Thanks to you, he *lived* his last weeks.'

Grace's protests that she'd just been doing her job had been ignored as she was enfolded in a crushing hug.

'I'm not catching a flight. I'm staying,' Grace said now, dragging out a chair and slumping into it.

'You are?'

'He—Salvatore—he's left me half of everything.'

The older woman clamped a hand to her mouth, her eyes as big as saucers above her fingers, staring at Grace.

'I told him—the lawyer—that I couldn't accept. That it wouldn't be proper. He said that *he*—' her eyes narrowed into contemptuous slits '—the son—Theo—apparently wants to buy me out. He has offered a crazy amount of money. I don't want money, Marta. I don't want anything!' she wailed, her voice shaking with emotion.

'Oh, I know that. Everyone here does. *We* all know you, Grace, but I suppose Theo thinks it's such an ancient place, with so much history, that it should stay in the family?' the older woman suggested apologetically.

Grace nodded her agreement. 'I thought that too, and I said he could have it, obviously. Even though he sounds like—'

She bit her tongue and gave a weak smile, thinking, *Suck it up, Grace*. Inexplicably—or at least it was to her—the palazzo staff never badmouthed the absent son.

Grace had her own opinion when it came to Theo Ranieri, who had never *once* visited his dying father, and not even come to the funeral, but she kept it to herself.

'Theo is not poor. You should not give it away.'

Grace's soft mouth hardened. 'I don't intend to. He wants to buy me out, but only so—' angry tears sprang to her blue eyes '—so that he can sell everything! I can't believe that anyone could be so— It's as if he wants to erase everything his father loved! His heritage!' Her soft lips quivered. 'How can he—?' she began. Then she stopped and, making a supreme effort to contain her surging emotions, shook her head.

The housekeeper had gone pale. 'I was afraid of something like this,' she admitted.

'Don't worry. I won't let him. I can stop him,'

Grace gritted, tucking the lint-pale strands of hair she had dislodged behind her ears. 'And I will. If I say no—if I live here—he can't sell. And I do say no.'

The older woman looked doubtful; her hand shook as she poured fresh coffee into her cup. 'Theo could always be very stubborn when he made up his mind...'

'So can I,' Grace promised grimly.

'It is so sad that it has come to this.'

Sad? Grace thought. It was totally *outrageous*! And that was a mild way of expressing her feelings.

She had no idea what had caused the relationship between father and son to break down, and although curious she had never considered it her place to ask. Even now things had changed, still she couldn't make herself ask.

Why does he hate his father so much?

Surely indifference could not explain his behaviour?

'Perhaps Salvatore suspected what his son would do? And the will was his way of...? Well, whatever the reason,' she added, her narrow shoulders lifting as she accepted the cup of coffee Marta pushed her way, 'his son can't sell if I say no and live here.' Her blue eyes sparked with a militant light. 'And I *do* say no. He can't sell! This place, the palazzo, the estate, the *peo-*

ple,' she declared fiercely. 'It was Salvatore's life, and I won't let his son destroy it! I'm moving in and I'm not budging.'

CHAPTER TWO

STRAIGHT AFTER SHE had handed in her notice
to the nursing agency Grace had emailed her
parents to let them know that she wouldn't be
coming home. She had included the bare bones
of the situation and then sat back to wait for her
phone to ring. Finally it had, and now she was
sitting talking online to her entire family, who
were crowded into her parents' booklined sitting room.

So far Simon, her lawyer brother, had suggested that the son might stand a good chance
of breaking the will, warning that it could get
vicious and asking what drugs Salvatore had
been on.

'Could the son say he was—?'

Grace immediately saw where he was going
and cut across him. 'He remained as sharp as
you or me, right up to the end.'

'All right…no need to get het-up. I'm just
covering the possibilities.'

'I'm sure you're a very good lawyer, Simon, but you're also my brother.'

Her psychiatrist brother Rob cut in. 'Exactly. Grace needs a bit of support.' Before she could be grateful, he added, 'Were you sleeping with the old guy? Not that I'm judging… I've seen photos. He was good-looking for an old guy.'

Well, if he wasn't judging he'd be the only one, Grace thought grimly. The manager at the agency had made a couple of very pointed comments concerning vulnerable elderly patients and ethics.

Now it was her sister's turn, and it was almost a relief when Hope seemed mostly interested in this inconvenience to her own social calendar.

Grace leaned back from the computer screen as her sister leaned in so close that if she'd had a blemish it would have showed. It didn't, because there was a reason her sister never argued when people complimented her on her perfect skin—she *did* have perfect skin.

Hope, with her supermodel looks, had perfect everything.

She also had the only man that Grace had ever loved.

Grace sometimes asked herself if she *still* loved George…if that was the reason that she'd not had a proper boyfriend since him?

George hadn't changed at all, except he no longer had the cute floppy fringe that Grace had fallen in love with, or the gap between his front teeth which her sister had insisted on being eliminated for the wedding photographs.

'But you *have* to come home, Grace. George and I are having our weekend in Paris—you know that.'

Behind her, her husband waved and looked apologetic. He had looked apologetic when he'd told her he was in love with her sister, but that he still loved her just *like* a sister. He'd seemed to think this would be some sort of compensation.

It hadn't been.

'I've been so busy with the new series. And in case anyone is interested, I'm exhausted—and George is simply off-the-scale stressed.'

'I'm not really….'

His wife ignored him.

'Grace, you promised to babysit. You know we can't leave Artie with anyone else but you. He's so sensitive. And, well, Aria is being *totally* intransigent,' she said, pouting as she referenced their incredible nanny. 'I'm sure her sister would understand if she wasn't there for the wedding.'

'Sorry.' Grace bit her well-bitten tongue. Artie with his sunny smile was gorgeous, and maybe the *easiest* baby on the planet, but she wasn't going to be budged.

'Hope, not everything is about you.'

This online defence came from a most unexpected direction—her mum.

'This is a massive opportunity for your sister. She doesn't have a career—'

'I do have—'

'She doesn't have a partner. I think that she's being very sensible to stay put and show she's not a pushover. It's a very good tactic to up the price. Try not to be such a people-pleaser, Grace. Stand up for yourself.'

Grace sighed. It was rare that she received approval from either of her parents, and the only reason she was now was because they had mistaken her motives. They really thought that her staying put was some sort of 'possession is nine-tenths of the law' negotiating move.

'Good girl, Grace,' said her father, looking just as distinguished as he did on the cover of his latest bestseller.

Modesty forbade him from mentioning that he had held the number one slot on the non-fiction bestseller list for eight weeks last year—well, not mentioning it often…and then only casually.

'Just don't let this guy intimidate you. I'm looking him up as we speak. He's brilliant, of course, but he's got a reputation for being pretty ruthless and manipulative. I could come over… back you up…'

'I don't want a better price, Dad. I'm not interested in the money. And Salvatore's death is not an o*pportunity*—'

'Of course not, darling. Take the moral high ground,' her mother interrupted. 'Sincerity is *so* you. But a person has to be practical in life— especially someone with no prospects. You have no idea how much we both worry about you in the future, when we're gone.'

The image of her energetic mother, who rose at five a.m. every day to work out and refused to allow white bread in the house, being on her last legs made Grace bite back a laugh. Her anger faded as her sense of the ridiculousness of the situation reasserted itself. She had decided a long time ago that she loved her family, and that the best way to cope with them and not fall out with them when they tried to be 'encouraging' was to consider them a comedy act: a very tall, good-looking, talented comedy act.

Sometimes she felt like a Shetland pony in a family of thoroughbreds…

'I really don't think that's imminent, Mum. And as for taking care of myself—I left home when I was eighteen.'

The moment the words left her lips she knew

it had been a bad move to bring up the still-sensitive subject of her leaving home.

Turning down a place at Oxford in favour of a place on a nursing degree course in London had not quite caused her family to disown her, but it had been close. She loved them dearly, but there was no doubt they were a bunch of high-achieving intellectual snobs. Though she also knew that if she was ever in any real trouble they'd be there for her.

'I'm really not interested in money,' she tacked on quickly. 'Oh, gosh... I think I'm losing you...'

She cut the connection and didn't feel even slightly guilty.

Theo loosened his tie, and a moment later it joined his jacket on the back seat of his car. He had driven direct from the Florence office to the palazzo. Though these days he was based mainly in the States and the UK, he had retained his original Italian base.

It was a journey he had not made since he was an angry eighteen-year-old, and then it had been in the opposite direction, his mode of transport his feet and his thumb, his fuel anger.

He remembered the exhilaration of finally being free. He'd been counting down the days to severing all connections since that fateful day he'd discovered what his father was. Thanks to attending boarding school in England, he had only been home for the holidays. When he could he had spent them with friends, but when forced to return home to the palazzo he had studiously ignored his father. Instead he would head out into the hills every day, either alone or with Nico, the estate manager's son, who hated it there as much as he had.

The anger was still there, but there was no shoe leather involved today. Instead the silent growl of an electric engine that powered the convertible.

Theo had vowed that day he'd never set foot in the place again. He'd told his ashen-faced father that now he was an adult, and had a choice, it was no longer his home.

Yet here he was.

He resented the necessity and the reason for that necessity. One Grace Stewart. When his legal team had told him that she wouldn't sell he had been irritated, and instructed them to find out what she wanted and give it to her.

They had come back with the news that she didn't want anything—which he didn't believe. Everyone had a price, and this woman would be no exception.

The slim file that had landed in his inbox had not suggested she was any different, just possibly slightly more boring. There was certainly nothing that could be used as leverage against her in the file. Though to be certain he had employed Rollo Eden to dig a little deeper.

Theo did not particularly *like* Rollo, but liking was not necessary. It was thanks to the private investigator's digging ability that they had not lost a multimillion-dollar contract. The man had outed the mole in their midst who was passing on information to a rival firm. So what if he got near the line sometimes? While he stayed just the right side of it and produced results Theo would continue to utilise his skills when required, with no qualms.

This task was a little below his pay grade, but when Theo had explained the situation he had agreed to handle it personally and not pass it on.

But Theo was not hanging around waiting for Rollo to deliver. He had put a plan into action. Initially he had thought about speaking directly to the little gold-digger, and then another solution had come to him, brilliant in its simplicity.

If she wouldn't move out, he'd move in— which could cramp her style when it came to entertaining. She probably fancied herself as chatelaine of a castle, he concluded scornfully.

If he couldn't sell up without her agreement, the reverse was also true. If she had any plans that involved the estate she'd have to run them past him, and she would find him not co-operative.

Despite the amused smile that played around his lips at the thought, he felt the tension climb into his shoulders. He knew that once he turned the next bend the palazzo would be in view. He couldn't think of it as home any longer—it had stopped being his home the day of his mother's funeral. He'd been so angry with her for leaving him. And then, quite by accident, he had discovered from his hiding place the reason she had left him, and his anger had shifted to the person responsible.

He found his foot easing off the accelerator, delaying the moment of his first glimpse of the iconic view that was replicated in innumerable books on the architectural gems of Tuscany. Whether approaching by helicopter or car, guests arriving were guaranteed a catch-your-breath moment.

The palazzo was built on the site of the original monastic building that had been the dream of an ancestor of his in the sixteenth century. Its classic proportions still incorporated an old clock tower and the original ecclesiastical buildings, spread around the main palazzo like a village.

In his mind, he visualised the massive Renaissance gates which marked the point when a visitor would be hit by the full spectacle of the place. Driving along the tree-lined avenue and upwards towards the palazzo the visitor would be surrounded by tier after tier of immaculate flower-bedecked manicured gardens, intersected by stone walkways and statuary, rising to the final level that stopped short of a cliff face that opened on to the azure ocean.

Aware of the heavy thud of his heart, and refusing to acknowledge it, he veered the car off the dusty track and pulled up with a screech of brakes and a cloud of dust onto the grassy verge.

He told himself that he had stopped to stretch his legs, but the self-delusion was a single cell thin when he opened the door and was hit by the pungent, warm and earthy signature scent that he had never forgotten. It immediately filled his nostrils as his feet hit the pine-needle-strewn floor.

He didn't want to admit even to himself how the familiarity unsettled him—how being *here* unsettled him. He hadn't been prepared to feel this way, and it was all that damned woman's fault.

He had moved on. The death of the father he had rejected had been the final closure of a chapter—the closure that would be complete when he sold his heritage.

The only thing standing in the way was the woman who had got her claws into his father. Well, like they said, there was no fool like an old fool...

Not that his father had been old, as such—sixty-five was nothing these days, and his father had died three days short of that birthday.

Theo had learnt after the fact of his death, from the lawyers. The cold, clinical words of the email had stared up at him.

Regret to inform...dead...lost his brave fight...

It had taken Theo a while to connect the words—for the clichés to make sense. There had been no forewarning. Had his estranged father considered reaching out when he'd known the end was near?

And if he had...?

Theo gave an internal shrug, pushing away the question. Such speculation was pointless. His father had not reached out—except, perhaps, he mused cynically, to his opportunist nurse, who had been his 'companion' in his dying weeks and months.

No, he would do better focusing on the obstacle in his path than on the emotions that had been shaken loose by his father's death, he decided, his thoughts turning to the gold-digger.

His pride was insulted by the idea of anyone thinking they could shake him down.

Maybe she thought it was a case of like father like son?

If so, she would soon discover this was not the case.

He was retracing his steps when he heard the sound. He paused, frowning as he listened, remembering the encounter he'd once had with a wild boar in almost this exact spot.

It was most likely a deer.

Then he heard it again. Not a deer, or a wild boar. Unless they could swear.

Grace was not lost—just slightly off course.

She knew exactly where she was, and she also knew that her directional miscalculation by the stream after that slip had put an extra mile on her morning hike.

A mile would not be an issue if she hadn't turned her ankle...

At least the headache she had woken up with this morning had cleared. Or maybe she couldn't feel it above the throb from her ankle.

She paused, leaning on the fallen branch that made a useful crutch. Her full lower lip caught between her teeth, she bent forward, her determined optimism faltering as she unwrapped the tee shirt she had dipped in the icy stream and wrapped it around her injured extremity to relieve her ankle. Despite her make-do cold compress her ankle was already puffy, starting to discolour, and three times the size of the other.

'It looks worse than it is,' she told herself, without conviction.

From where he stood in the tree line, Theo scanned the injured ankle with clinical detachment. A detachment that soon evaporated, morphing into something less objective as his glance shifted, travelling upwards over the sinuous length of the woman's legs, reaching the understated feminine flare of hips emphasised by the narrowness of a waist that he estimated he could have spanned with his hands.

At that moment the who she was and the how she'd got here became of secondary importance to the way one strap of the vest she was wearing had slid down over a smooth shoulder, revealing a lot of the sports bra she wore underneath. A trickle of sweat was winding a slow path from the hollow at the base of her throat to the cleavage that without the bra would have been revealed.

He had an impression of the soft sounds of nature around them fading out as his eyes followed the slow progress of that pearl of moisture over her pale skin, its journey resulting in a flash of heat that settled solidly in his groin.

For a self-indulgent moment Theo allowed his libido to flare unchecked, welcoming the distraction, taking in the slim curves, the slender, elegant neck, the pale almost silver hair that stuck to her face and spilled untidily down her back.

'It looks pretty bad.'

At the sound of his voice, the woman started like a deer, her head coming up just in time to witness Theo materialising out of the trees.

The electric blue of those wide, scared eyes lifted to his brought Theo to a dead halt as his body was jolted by a fresh sexual charge.

The adrenaline dumped in Grace's bloodstream screamed fight or flight—only flight was not an option. A fact she didn't fully realise until she had scrambled to her feet.

Crying out in pain, she balanced on one leg, her eyes never leaving the man who towered over her for one second as she raised her branch defensively to warn him off. She maintained her stork-like pose for as long as it took her to snatch a deep breath—before she promptly fell on her bottom.

Between losing her balance and hitting the

ground she put a name to the face of the sinister stranger.

This was Theo Ranieri.

There were younger, less threatening versions of the palazzo's joint owner in framed photos throughout the palazzo, but even if there hadn't been she would have recognised him. Long before she'd arrived here she'd seen an interview in which he had memorably verbally eviscerated the cocky reporter who had made the mistake of coming ill prepared when he'd been granted an interview.

The recognition came to her in a lightbulb moment—a little like the way your life was meant to flash before your eyes when you were dying.

Except she wasn't dying—or only of mortification.

On the plus side, she was no longer gut-freezingly terrified. Not that her thundering heart had responded to this information yet. Her breath was still coming far too fast to cope with her raised pulse.

'That must have hurt.'

Grace eased herself onto one hip and lifted her ankle off the floor, raising her chin and aiming for a defiant 'don't mess with me' angle.

Some of the defiance slid into something messier and more confusing as her eyes meshed with his dark stare. Shading her eyes with one protective hand, she shook back her hair, most of which had escaped the loose knot it had been gathered in on the back of her neck.

'I'm fine,' she gritted out through clenched teeth, dragging a hand across her sweaty damp face, oblivious to the dusty smear it left.

In the flesh, Theo Ranieri was more of everything he appeared to be in photographs or on the screen. Looking up at him made her feel quivery, light-headed and hot. But that was the pain, she told herself. That and a reaction to that split-second of visceral fear she had experienced when he had appeared out of nowhere.

Someone that big ought to make more noise, she decided resentfully as her eyes swept upwards from his dusty leather shoes over his long legs. The cut of his tailored trousers did not disguise the strength of his muscular thighs. His hips were narrow in comparison to the width of his powerful shoulders, and through the white of his shirt she could see a faint shadow suggestive of body hair.

She polished her righteous indignation to distract herself from the little sexual quiver in the pit of her belly that was a result of the earthy male image he presented.

Even without the vulnerability factor of the setting, Theo Ranieri possessed a raw physical presence that would intimidate and overpower in an air-conditioned crowded room. But somehow he didn't seem out of place in the raw, natural environment. He seemed part of it.

His features were undeniably perfect. The slant of his high cheekbones, the aquiline blade of his nose, his thickly delineated jet brows and his dark, almost black stare were not softened in any way by the crazily long lashes that framed his deep-set eyes. The fuller curve of his lower lip contrasted with the firmness of the upper, but it did not give his mouth a feminine softness, rather a disturbingly sensual provocation and a hint of cruelty.

He raised one dark brow and she brought her lashes down in a protective sweep. He probably took being stared at as his due, but she was damned if she was going to feed his no doubt massive ego.

Ironically, for weeks she had rehearsed the cutting comments she'd like to deliver to Salvatore's callous son if she ever had the opportunity, knowing that because of her profession she never would. But now professional standards no longer applied to her position, and he was here at the mercy of her tongue. She could confront him with his callous treatment of his dying father. A man who had deserved so much better.

Here was the opportunity to put her emotions into words without bawling her head off. But not, it turned out, the ability. Her feelings had solidified into a painful, inarticulate lump in her throat. If she knew one thing, she knew that this was a man she didn't want to cry in front of.

'I'm fine,' she lied, sounding cranky and slightly breathless.

'Debatable…' he drawled, sounding more amused than concerned. 'You've rung someone?'

'I forgot my phone.' The admission came through clenched teeth.

'Careless.'

She found herself hating his drawl. 'It's fine. I happen to live very close.'

She held his eyes with a pretence of cool composure which, considering she was sitting on the dirt floor, looking and for that matter feeling as though she had been dragged through several hedges backwards, was an achievement that deserved applause.

His right eyebrow joined the left, nearly hitting his hairline, then suddenly levelled as she saw a fractional widening of his dark eyes before the glitter of recognition appeared.

'*You're* Grace Stewart?'

* * *

Theo felt a surge of irritation the moment the redundant question left his lips. He considered himself intellectually agile, but he did not make assumptions. And yet he had.

Though if someone had thought to include a photograph in the pathetically thin file he had read, he would not have previously been thinking boring and average. The woman sitting on the forest floor, glaring up at him with eyes so searingly shockingly blue, was neither average nor boring. The skin under the smears of dirt had a pale clarity that seemed to glow in the shaded light.

This discovery required some rapid mental readjustment—which was not easy when his libido kept escaping its leash. Maybe it was like father, like son?

His jaw hardened at the thought as he rejected any and all comparisons with his father. Unlike his late parent, he had never pretended to be a saint and he was not a cheat. He had never promised a woman anything, never made vows and broken them, forcing a woman he claimed to love to the point of utter black despair where she saw no way back.

'What are you doing here anyway?'

The accusing words brought his attention

back to the moment and to the figure sitting at his feet. 'Did I need to ask permission?'

His sarcasm pushed colour into her pale cheeks. 'I mean I— We had no idea you were coming. A bit of warning might have been nice.'

It sounded petulant and she felt stupid—especially as she was not exactly operating from a position of authority and was actually on her behind!

'Just checking you haven't stolen the silver.'

His lazy mockery touched a nerve and burnt like acid. Her chin went up. 'Very funny.' Then the very real mortifying possibility that he wasn't joking hit her. 'Half of it is mine,' she countered observing from the flare of his nostrils that he hadn't liked that. Well, good—she was glad.

The glare on glare, blue on black contest went on for what to Grace felt like a lifetime before he broke the silence.

'Are you going to stay there all day, or do you want a lift?'

She blinked. Of course he hadn't just materialised. He had a car.

'Or there is always the option, painful though it might be, of crawling on your hands and knees.' His expressive brows twitched. 'Up to you.'

Her eyes narrowed. He wasn't as bad as she

had imagined he was going to be—he was much, *much* worse!

'I'll take the lift.'

But would she take the hand that was extended to her?

As she looked at those long brown square-tipped fingers, suddenly the crawling option did not seem so terrible...

Theo watched her regard his hand with the enthusiasm most people reserved for a striking snake. He could almost see her swallow and choke on her pride as finally she stretched out her hand to meet his.

His amusement faded as he captured her slender, pale and cold fingers in his and the resultant shock of sexual electricity made him catch his breath and clench his jaw against its unexpected intensity. The only comfort was the knowledge that she felt it too. He saw it in the shocked wide opening of her dramatic blue eyes.

Maybe she didn't like the idea of not being in control of a situation any more than he did?

Or maybe she was filing away the information to use to her advantage?

Breaking the connection the second she was able, Grace wiped her hand on the cotton of her light trousers.

'Thanks,' she mumbled, swaying as she tried to balance precariously on one leg, before she tentatively placed the injured foot lightly on the ground. Being on her feet gave her very little extra advantage—she was still staring at his mid chest area.

'How much damage have you done?' he asked, sounding impatient.

'It's just a sprain.' She didn't add that sprains could often be more troublesome than a break.

'You a doctor?'

'No, a nurse.'

'So you are…'

Grace caught the glint of anger in his dark eyes.

'A credit to your profession, I'm sure,' he drawled nastily.

'My *ex*-profession,' she said, to needle him. And it did.

'I am assuming you do want a lift back?'

She sighed, and responded with tight-lipped formality. 'That would be most kind, Mr…'

'I think under the circumstances you'd better make it Theo—'

'Circumstances?' she queried as he began to walk away.

'Well, we will be living together,' he tossed over his shoulder, smiling to himself.

'Live? With you? But I'm staying here—you live in England.'

She must have read his bio online.

'So do you,' he retorted, his sardonic smile fading into exaggeration as he watched her make her way towards him in a combination of clearly painful shuffles and hopping steps.

He swore under his breath.

She didn't register his intention until he strode across to her and swept her up into his arms with a casual display of strength.

'I am more than capable,' she said, holding herself stiff while finding the depth and the intensity of her awareness of the hardness of his body, the warmth of his skin, deeply unsettling.

'I'd like to arrive sometime this year.'

She gave a sigh of relief when he set her down beside a gleaming monster of a car, opened the passenger door and left her to climb in as he walked around the vehicle to the driver's side.

By the time Grace had managed to clamber awkwardly in he was already seated and waiting.

'It's not far,' she said, and immediately felt stupid.

Like he doesn't know the way!

'Directions?' he said, seeming to enjoy her discomfort.

'Are you serious?' she asked as the car drew onto the road.

'About what? Directions? No, I remember the way.'

'You're not really going to be staying here?'

He flashed her a quick malicious smile. 'It's a big house. I'm sure we'll rub along nicely.'

CHAPTER THREE

ONCE THEY DREW up outside the porticoed entrance to the palazzo he unbelted and without looking at her spoke in a brusque voice, his eyes trained on the building.

'I'll send someone out for you.'

As if she was a parcel, Grace thought indignantly.

Before she could respond, he had vanished inside.

Grace had made her own slow and painful way as far as the shallow flight of steps that led to the massive metal-banded oak door when someone appeared. It was Marta, looking more flushed than normal.

'Oh, you poor thing! How lucky that Theo found you.'

Grace's lips tightened. She made it sound as though he'd been looking for her.

'Sure, he's my hero,' she said, accepting the arm the older woman placed around her waist

and obeying the instruction to lean on Marta
with gratitude.

Marta seemed oblivious to her sarcasm as
she supported Grace up the steps and through
the open door.

'We have rung the doctor.'

'That really isn't necessary.'

'Theo said we should.'

'I don't care what *Theo* says. I don't want
a doctor.' She saw the hurt, shocked expression on the housekeeper's face and stretched
her lips into a smile. 'All a doctor would say is
use a cold compress, elevate my leg and take
painkillers.'

'Theo—'

Oh, give me strength, Grace thought, biting
back a retort as thoughts of a lifetime of living with people who thought they knew better
came into play.

'Fine.'

The older woman looked approving, then
doubtful when Grace grabbed the edge of the
banister on the curving dramatic staircase that
dominated the massive hall.

'I'll get someone to carry you.'

'Really, no. I'm fine.' Grace gave a cheery
smile to show just how fine she was.

'Well…all right. Isn't it marvellous that Theo
is finally home?'

The woman was serious, Grace realised, and there were tears in her eyes.

'Marvellous,' Grace echoed drily, thinking it would have been a hell of a lot more marvellous if he'd been home in time to say goodbye to his father.

Once she had hobbled up and around the first curve of the staircase, and was confident she was out of sight, Grace sat down and shuffled on her bottom the rest of the way up to her first-floor room. It wasn't the most elegant way of doing things, but compared with the alternative of being carried...

The memory of the recent occasion was too fresh to run the risk of a repeat.

An almost tactile image of long brown fingers pressed lightly against her back was so vivid that in the act of pulling herself to her feet with the aid of the banister she almost fell back down again.

When he arrived, the doctor approved the treatment she had prescribed herself and suggested a supportive bandage when she got out and about again.

After he had left Grace resisted the temptation to say *I told you so* to Marta as the woman fussed around. Actually, if she was honest, being fussed over had a certain novelty value, coming as she did from a family who didn't do cosseting. Tea and sympathy wasn't a thing for the Stewart clan—they just sucked it up and got on with it.

'Such a shame,' Marta said when she'd checked for the umpteenth time that Grace had everything she needed, 'that you can't join Theo for dinner on his first night here.'

'Oh, God, no!' Grace exclaimed without thinking, then moderated her response by looking at her elevated foot, swathed in ice packs. 'It would be too painful,' she said.

'Of course,' the other woman agreed, obviously pacified by her explanation, leaving Grace mystified as to why people who had loved Salvatore appeared so happy to see his hateful son.

How could they forgive him?

Mass hypnosis, maybe?

Grace got her first text from Nic, the estate manager, an hour later. She frowned and sent him a quick one back.

I'm sure it's just a misunderstanding.

Two hours and five texts later it was clear even to Grace, who was not on top of the details, that they were not dealing with a simple misunderstanding. The bank was apparently blocking payments to their suppliers.

That would stop work on the new olive press, because the suppliers were refusing to deliver. And the progress on the renovations of some of the buildings intended to become eco-tourist accommodation had been halted because the delivery of marble from the local quarry had been cancelled.

Both had been pet projects that Salvatore had taken her to see, and there were several other similar projects.

'It's almost as if someone is deliberately sabotaging us,' Nic observed, his frustration at the situation obvious.

Grace had gradually become relaxed around Nic and lowered her defences, mentally filing him as one of the good guys. Maybe it was because his mother was English. She didn't self-censor before she closed her eyes and swore.

'Don't worry, I'll sort it—'

'Just leave it with me and call it a day,' she said. The face she saw reflected back from the mirror on the opposite wall was set and grimly unfamiliar. 'Go home to your family.'

Salvatore, she thought, with an emotional little mental gulp, had always remembered Nic's children's names. For the first time she was struck—*really* struck—by the weight of responsibility that her inheritance had placed on her, the trust that Salvatore had placed *in* her.

'It's late. I'll get back to you in the morning.'

Pushing aside the supper tray that she had not touched—she had just moved the food around to make it look as though she had—Grace kicked off the ice packs and eased herself out of bed, muttering to herself. She fought her way into the robe slung across the bottom of the bed and then, grabbing the silver-handled cane that Marta had produced earlier, paused to swallow a couple of the painkillers before making her way out into the corridor.

She half slid down the stairs, leaning on the smooth banister, too angry to register the discomfort in her ankle. As it turned out, anger was the best anti-inflammatory on the market.

Leaning on the cane, she went in search of her quarry, her anger getting hotter with every step.

When she reached Salvatore's study the door was open. She paused, her heart thudding, and then felt angry at her caution in hesitating. She pushed the door wider and stepped inside. The lights above the portrait of Salvatore's late wife illuminated the painting of the beautiful woman and cast shadows around the empty room.

Her search progressed.

The chandeliers in the drawing room were

lit, but it was empty too. She hobbled across to look through the French doors, but there was no tall figure outside in the moonlight.

The smaller salon was empty too.

As Grace turned to walk along the adjoining corridor, she wondered what people would say if they saw her—then laughed, because nobody was going ask her what she was doing. She didn't work here. She wasn't a visitor. She belonged. The palazzo was hers and she was not going to let anyone drive her out.

Because that was what he was trying to do.

She felt stupid for not realising it immediately.

The door to the smaller dining room where she normally ate was open, light spilling out, along with the sound of a piano playing a soft, heart-squeezing melody.

She pushed the door further open, taking in at a glance the half-burnt candles on the table, the bottle of wine, half full, an empty glass—this was definitely a half-empty day—and a plate.

The figure seated at the piano in the corner had his eyes closed, his fingers moving across the keys. He seemed oblivious to her presence.

The music was ineffably sad. It made Grace think of the eyes of that portrait in the study. How long had she been dead? Had her son known her? Grace had never asked, and nobody spoke about her or the circumstances of her death.

She started as the music stopped and his fingers came down with a discordant crash on the keys. The stool scraped the floor as Theo got to his feet, tall and elegant, in a black shirt open at the neck and black tailored trousers.

Grace despised herself for the quivering awareness that she felt like a dark itch under her skin. Although, in her defence, she really couldn't see how any woman could not be sexually aware of him.

'Are you looking for me? For food?' One dark brow lifted to a sardonic angle. 'Or are you here to broker a deal?'

'I'm looking for you,' she said, not lowering her gaze and fixing him with a steady blue stare.

'Should you be on your feet?' Theo asked.

They were, he noticed, bare. And the robe she was wearing was long enough to trip her up, and gave the impression she was floating. Cinched in tight at the waist, it was the same blue as her eyes.

He found himself wondering what, if anything, she had on underneath, and thought about running his fingers through the fine strands of blonde hair that fell around her face like a silky curtain, framing the oval of her face.

It was no longer a mystery why his father had left her a fortune. It was easy to see how an elderly, vulnerable man would have fallen for the combination of wide-eyed, wholesome sincerity with a core of sensuality.

He felt the sharp stab of desire, and wished he hadn't ended things with Cleo so abruptly. He was neither elderly, nor vulnerable, but celibacy didn't suit him. It never had.

He didn't need a companion, he needed sex—but not with this woman.

'Your concern is touching,' she said, making her voice cold and refusing to be distracted by the way he was staring at her.

He pushed his hands into his pockets and sauntered towards her. She wanted to yell, *Stop there!* but didn't. Because that would have meant she was scared of him—which she wasn't.

Not of him...but maybe of the feelings he was shaking free inside her?

Turning a deaf ear to the idea, she stuck out her chin.

'So now you've found me what do you want to do with me?'

The purred question sent a rush of blood to

her cheeks. She mentally sidestepped the issue of what she'd like to do with him the same way she would have an unexplored bomb in her path.

'I've had some phone calls from Nic.' Despite her efforts to stay calm her voice now shook with anger.

'You have your boyfriend well trained.'

'Nic is the estate manager,' she bit back.

His brow momentarily furrowed but then smoothed. 'After my time.'

During his time the estate manager had been Luis who, even though he must have been a nuisance, had allowed him to tag along with him and his son, who coincidentally had been called Nico...

'He's been manager eight years.'

His smile held no humour. 'Like I said, after my time,' he said, watching her full lips attempt to pinch into an expression of disapproval their plump generosity was not constructed for. The thought of what those lips were perfectly constructed for slipped past his mental shield, and his focus blurred as a testosterone hit made itself felt.

'Nic has not had a good day. There have been issues—several issues. Cancelled deliveries, payments not going through… Do you know anything about that?'

'I am not cut out to be a silent partner,' he said.

He hadn't even tried to deny it.

'Neither—' she flung back '—am I!'

She paused and tried to gather the frayed ends of her fast-unravelling temper.

'I don't understand…why would you do this?' she asked, genuinely mystified by this level of malice.

'Why do you care?' he countered.

'The projects you are attempting to sabotage were important to your father.' Scanning his face for any sign that her words had had any impact on him, she saw only a flinty stare for her troubles. 'Everyone is working so hard to make them happen because of your father. I—I promised.'

Biting her quivering lip and blinking hard, she opened her mouth to continue and then stopped, a look of horrified suspicion spreading across her face.

'Is that why you're doing this? Out of spite? He's dead,' she reminded him, deciding she had imagined his flinch. 'You can't hurt him any more. Why did you hate him so much?'

The words were out before she could stop

them—not that he appeared to register the question.

'The point isn't why…it's more the fact that I *can* do this.'

It did not escape her notice that he didn't deny her suggestion.

'Just as you can stop me selling off the land,' he continued heavily, '*I* can stop your little projects.'

He paused, watching her face grow pale and her blue eyes fly wide with a display of shock that might have been convincing if he hadn't known that she had smiled his father out of a fortune.

'Have you actually read any of the figures?' he asked her. 'Or did you just sign off on them?'

'Of course I read them. I'm not an idiot!' Grace flared indignantly. 'And if you had bothered to do your research,' she bit back, her scorn equal to his, 'you'd know it makes sound financial sense to pay those so-called *inflated* prices. Yes, I am aware that you can source marble for a quarter of the price we are paying, but it would be an inferior product. And, most importantly—'

Her lips tightened in annoyance as Theo cut across her before she could complete her explanation.

'I suppose you're on top of the projected labour costs for this—what was it?—olive press? Who is it pocketing the money on that rip-off? It isn't even very inventive.'

Grace had now gone paper-white with temper. 'You can cast slurs on me if you want—I don't care. But the people who work here deserve more respect. They deserve more than to be pawns in this childish payback. You can stamp your foot because you don't get your own way, but don't libel people who are just doing their job.'

She folded her arms across her chest and flung him a look of simmering contempt.

'Do you know how *pathetic* that is?'

Grace saw the shock on his face at her contempt, but the shock of being ripped into that way quickly morphed into anger that turned his dark, flinty eyes into black ice.

'You will not speak to me in that manner!' he grated.

'Wanna bet?' she drawled, too angry to be cautious in the face of his white-lipped fury. 'And how about a few more facts for you? As I was saying about the marble—' she flung the word out like a challenge '—agreed, you *could* get it cheaper. But *this* marble is sourced locally, and it will give the local supplier and in turn local tradesmen jobs. It is authentic to the restoration, there will be no air miles involved getting it on site, and even if *you* don't care about that, other people do. You understand money?' she went on. 'Fine. Then you'll recognise good marketing. Those labour costs you think are too high? Those men you dismiss? They are highly skilled stonemasons…they're artisans, local talent. It's all about using skills that could be lost and the people who will stay in those restored buildings. If even half of them understand that, *like* that, it will be worth it, and long term we will recoup the costs!'

By the end of her tirade his anger had turned into amazement. Not just at her knowledge, but her apparent passion.

Could it be genuine?

He dismissed the possibility. With a woman like her there would always be an angle.

'How the hell do you know all this?' he asked.

Grace took a deep, steadying breath, feeling shaky in the aftermath of her emotional outburst. A lifetime with her charming, infuriating family had taught her that being confrontational was not a solution, and she prided herself on the fact that these days she reacted to provocation with calm reason.

But then she had never encountered Theo and his sneering until now.

'I'm interested,' she responded, struggling belatedly to lower the emotional temperature of the conversation. 'Because passion can be contagious, and your father was passionate about these projects.'

A slow, sad smile spread across her face.

'He had so much knowledge and enthusiasm. He was so— Oh, God!'

She broke off as her chest heaved and a sob bubbled up. She pressed her hand to her mouth to hold it in.

'He was such a lovely man and I miss him,' she mumbled.

He could have destroyed the idealised image she had apparently built up of his father in one brutal sentence.

So why didn't he?

Because he told himself it didn't matter what this woman's relationship with his father was— or rather had been. It didn't matter if she was genuine or a brilliant actress. He needed to focus on the fact that she was here and she stood in his way. Anything else was a distraction.

'Well, he's not here. But I am. And a few

tears and an appeal to my eco-credentials are not going to work on me. If you want my signature you have to give me sound financial reasons.'

At the brutal words her head came up. Eyes still shining with unshed tears, she flicked her hair back and glared at him.

'I thought I had.'

Damn her.

She had.

'You're actually a horrible man!'

Not very original, but indisputably accurate.

How, she wondered, remembering the music she had heard him produce, could someone so cold and cruel play the piano with such emotional intensity?

'You have no idea how wounded I am by that.' He produced another of his uniquely unpleasant smiles from a mouth that was uniquely sensual. 'I thought someone in your job needed professional distance. Do you get broken up every time a patient dies? Or only over the ones who have left you a fortune?'

She regarded him with simmering dislike bright in her blue eyes. 'Actually, yes, I do struggle with retaining my detachment.'

And it did take a toll on her personally, that

inability to switch off after a long day when she'd become emotionally invested in a patient.

'But I'm a good nurse despite that.'

Though she knew there had been times when the objectivity that had eluded her would have made her a better nurse and also made her life a lot easier.

Her chest lifted in a silent sigh as she struggled for some of that elusive objectivity now.

'Not that I expect you to be particularly interested. Just as I'm not interested in whether you are naturally unpleasant or you're simply working at it. But I am assuming that you believe if you're unpleasant enough…if you throw enough roadblocks in my way… I'll just roll over?'

She raised her well-defined feathery brows, despite the fact that her internal temperature had shot into the red danger zone, and she forced her blue stare to hold his for several cool moments before the tug of his mouth got the better of her.

That sculpted, sensual outline was exerting an unhealthy and disturbing fascination for her.

'I'm staying put,' she told him. 'You can be as vile and unpleasant as you like. I won't allow you to destroy Palazzo della Stellato.'

Theo reared back his dark head in shock as she went on the offensive. This was not going as he had planned.

The knot of frustration in his chest tightened. There was not a shred of compromise in the challenging blue gaze that so coolly held his. The pulse kicking wildly at the base of her throat and her clenched fists were the only outward indication that she was not as calm as she appeared.

'What is your problem, anyway?' she demanded. 'Why do you want to destroy everything? Your father only ever said what a marvellous person you are…he was proud of you!'

He gave a smile of brilliant insincerity as he took a step towards her…

The equally strong instincts that were urging her to step towards him and retreat cancelled each other out, and Grace stayed where she was, her feet glued to the spot, her heart thudding painfully in her chest…

'You have no idea how much I am looking forward to more cosy chats like this, *cara*,' he drawled, veiling his eyes with long lashes, concealing the flash of shock in their dark depths as he realised that the long fingers of his right hand seemed to be acting on some automatic setting and had found their way to her jaw.

A frown flickered across his brow. His intention had been to break the contact—drop his hand as if her smooth skin stung—but before he could act on that intention he felt the quiver that ran through her body, felt the heat of her blue stare as she looked up at him, her breath coming in a series of quick, shallow little pants that lifted her breasts against the blue of her thin robe.

Theo prided himself on his logic, and on one level, separate from the sense-numbing streak of testosterone heat that immobilised him, his brain was functioning perfectly logically as it analysed the situation.

Yes, there was sexual attraction, a curiosity that was the elephant in the room. But it was a distraction, and unaddressed it would stay there, getting in the way. The best and most efficient way of dealing with it would be to stop wondering how she tasted and find out.

Kiss her and get it over with.

Kill the curiosity stone-dead and move on.

Startled blue eyes met his the moment before his head dipped...

Grace almost literally fell into his kiss.

The hand that slid to her waist was the only thing keeping her on her feet.

And then there was a slow, sensual, ever-deepening exploration as her lips moved across hers, his tongue probed, his tongue tasted…

Breathing hard, Theo drew back a second before his last shred of sanity was obliterated in the blast of heat that had been generated between them.

Grace forced her eyelids open, her gaze drifting to his face. She glimpsed emotions in his dark eyes that made her stomach muscles tighten painfully.

'Oh, Grace, here you are.'

Marta, oblivious to the atmosphere you could have sliced with a knife, bustled into the room, slim and efficient, her movements as neat as the hair coiled on her head.

Grace was so relieved she could have kissed the woman.

She had kissed the man.

She hadn't known kisses could be like that.

She really wished she still didn't, she decided.

Without looking up at him, she took a careful step away.

'If I'd known you wanted to eat down here I would have—'

'No,' Grace interrupted, in a slightly breath-

less voice. 'I just wanted to stretch my legs…
get a glass of milk.'

Learn a few things about raw sexual attraction I would have been happier staying ignorant of.

'You should have rung down,' the woman
chided, like a sleek, elegant mother hen.

'I should,' Grace agreed meekly.

She was thinking, *I should have done lots
of things…or rather should* not *have done one
specific thing.*

I don't suppose you'd give me a hand back
to my room?' She looked down at her foot and
didn't have to pretend to feel the throb that was
reasserting itself.

'Of course.'

Grace was very aware of the dark eyes that
followed her as she accepted Marta's supportive arm.

CHAPTER FOUR

To CLEAR HIS head after a restless night, Theo decided to go for a run. Without considering his route, he found himself on a path he remembered from his youth. It had once been worn down by his own feet. Now it was overgrown. At one point oak saplings had taken root, forcing him to make a short detour.

It would need to be cleared…

He almost immediately deleted this addition to his mental to-do list. It wouldn't need to be cleared because he wasn't staying. There wouldn't be other mornings when he ran to clear his head after a sleepless night.

It had been a mistake to come. But everyone made mistakes. The trick, he told himself, was living in the moment and never looking back, even though the uncomfortable voice in his head pointed out that looking back was what he was guilty of.

He upped his pace, even though the ground

underfoot was uneven and the path almost indistinguishable from the wild area it cut through. The mingled scent of the sea and the wild herbs underfoot filled his nostrils as he pushed on, losing the thread of his thought for a moment as he remembered the throaty little rasp deep in her throat as his tongue had encountered hers.

He narrowed his eyes as he began to run into the morning sun, dazzled for a second as he picked up his thought. The thing about mistakes was to own them and not repeat them... not beat yourself up over them.

He had, he told himself, acknowledged that the kiss was a mistake, and not one he was going to repeat.

But, *Dio*, it had been enjoyable!

Grace had not objected when her breakfast had been served in her room—actually, her ankle gave her the perfect excuse to stay there. She was briefly tempted, but then felt ashamed. She was not going to run away. *She* had done nothing wrong.

The implication that he *had*, and she was simply some innocent victim, brought a self-derisory furrow to her brow.

In her defence, Grace had not initiated the kiss. But the helpless plea really didn't work, and it made her impatient with herself. She hadn't exactly fought him off with a stick, she told herself scornfully. When she played the moment out in her head—which she had done more times than she could count—she could not have sworn, hand on heart, that she had not met him halfway.

The reality was he was the most *male* male she had ever encountered—and some part of her had responded to all that maleness. It was a weakness she hadn't known she possessed.

Was she going to hide?

The answer came as she unfolded her legs and pushed aside the breakfast tray balanced on the bed. She headed for the bathroom, noticing as she peeled off her nightdress that her ankle was feeling a lot better this morning. It was stiff, sore and colourful, certainly, but it took her weight without a problem, and she would be able to move around—albeit not with exactly fluid grace.

Her pain, she thought bitterly, was in her head. Where Theo had taken up residence!

The rebellion took her as far as the shower, before her inability to make a mess kicked in. She knew someone might be coming in to clean her room the moment she left, but in Grace's mind you cleared up your own stuff.

The nightdress was placed in the hamper

supplied for the purpose and she stepped into the shower—which was hot enough to make her step back before she hastily lowered the temperature.

She rarely applied make-up in the morning, and the fact she even thought about it today annoyed her. She was not out to impress anyone. It was enough to select a pair of cut-off jeans past their best, and a tee shirt that definitely said *I am not trying*.

Salvatore, always immaculately dressed, had breakfasted with her in the small dining room, selecting his breakfast from the silver dome-covered dishes along the sideboard. After one very uncomfortable lonely breakfast there after his death, Grace had opted to take her breakfast in the kitchen, sometimes with Marta.

Maybe, she mused, the old arrangement would be reinstated now Theo was in residence?

Grace had no intention of finding out. She headed for the kitchen, hoping to find Marta there.

She hovered a little around the door when it occurred to her that if Marta was there she might not be alone. God, it was too early to face that smug, supercilious smirk.

Bracing her slender shoulders, she stepped inside and found the room empty. Her shoulders

sagged and she despised the fact she was relieved—which was ridiculous. She didn't have
to hide away. This was her house and it was
about time she acted like it. There was nothing
Theo would enjoy more than seeing her creep-
ing around.

That defiance—or was it nervous apprehen-
sion?—gave her an appetite, and despite the
light breakfast she had already eaten in her
room Grace found herself unable to resist the
smell of freshly baked bread.

Just one slice, she told herself, heading for
the pantry—a massive slate-shelved space as
big as her parents' spacious kitchen.

She took a crusty loaf from the stone jar and
smothered it with a generous layer of butter,
before spooning some honey on top and heading with her coffee back to the table. She was
on her second bite when the door was flung
open and a figure dressed in black shorts and a
sweat-soaked vest that clung to an impressively
muscled torso burst into the room.

Grace's anticipation of that second bite vanished and the honey slid onto the plate.

Standing there, his hands braced on his muscular thighs, it was a couple of moment before
Theo straightened up and noticed her. He made
a noise in his throat that might have indicated
anything from revulsion to pleasure.

Grace deleted the latter possibility.

'Good run?' she asked brightly, trying and failing to ignore her physical reaction to him standing there in a vest, his skin steaming moistly.

In sharp tailoring it had been obvious he had an impressive body. Without it just how impressive became uncomfortably clear.

The muscle definition in his upper body was powerful, without being overly bulky. His legs were impossibly long, his hips narrow, his thighs powerful and dusted very lightly with dark hair that showed against the gleam of his skin.

Her stomach went into a series of painful and shaming somersaults and she let it, without feeling a shred of self-contempt. She was human and female. Even if he was a horrible man, with no redeeming features.

He stood there a moment, taking deep breaths that lifted his chest and sucked in the muscles of his flat belly, perfectly clear beneath the damp, clinging fabric. He might be horrible…but, God, he was hot and then some!

'Coffee?' she said casually, hitching one ankle over the other, hoping he'd say no because her knees were visibly shaking.

Grace was not thinking of anything above

her knees—it would be too embarrassing to examine in detail what was happening there.

After slinging her a look that wasn't friendly, but left her heart thudding, even though she didn't know why—a lot of her reactions to this man remained inexplicable—she watched as he walked across to the walk-in fridge, from where he extracted a jug of water. He filled a glass, swallowing the contents as he moved across to the old-fashioned range where a percolator bubbled.

He turned to Grace. 'Did you sleep well?'

'No.'

He sketched something approximating a smile that left his heavily lashed eyes dark and dangerous.

'Me neither.'

Reaching to the shelf above, he took a mug from the row and filled it.

She tried to avert her eyes from the taut, rippling movement of muscles in his shoulders and back. She was still staring when he turned around.

'Good run?' she asked.

'You already asked me.'

'I was being polite.' She bit back the childish addition that good manners were something he clearly knew nothing about.

'You sound nervous,' he said, watching her form under the sweep of his crazily long lashes.

Rather than deny it, she met his eyes levelly.

'Actually, I'm finding this situation quite… uncomfortable.' She felt the need to take another deep breath before adding, 'You own half the estate, and perhaps, technically,' she conceded, 'I should have consulted you before I made any decisions. Last night we left things unresolved, but to be honest—'

The sports watch he wore on his wrist caught the light, glinting metallically against his golden skin as he interrupted her with a sweeping gesture of one hand. 'By all means, let us be honest.'

Her lips tightened. 'You've not made any contact beyond trying to buy me out, and I didn't think you'd be interested in the day-to-day running of the estate,' she flung back.

'I'm not.'

Annoyance flared in her blue eyes. 'So you decided to be awkward just for the hell of it,' she responded, averting her eyes abruptly.

The rippling motion of the muscles in his brown throat worked as he swallowed the black coffee and created some rippling of her own inside her. He was one of those people who could make the most mundane action fascinating…

'So you want me to sign off on these projects?'

Her eyes narrowed. 'That depends on the price of your co-operation.'

Her eyes had flown to his face. They sank again now, and she felt the heat of shame rise in her cheeks as she thought of that kiss—a price that many women, she was sure, would be happy to pay.

'Hard negotiator...'

Her blue gaze lifted and her long lashes fanned across her cheeks as she loosed a peal of infectious laughter, thinking of what her family would make of that statement. Her family who, with an eye-roll, called her sentimental and a soft touch on all the occasions when it didn't suit them that she was.

'That's funny?'

She had a good laugh, he decided. Surprisingly deep and robust. It was actually bigger than she was.

Her delicacy made him feel like a bully, which he didn't like, and yet he had the impression she would have been offended at the idea he needed to make allowances for her physical fragility or her sex.

More tragic than funny, Grace decided with a noncommittal shrug. Because the truth was she loved her family, and she was more amused by their assumptions than crushed.

It suddenly occurred to her how at home Theo would feel with her family. They were all over-achieving thoroughbreds who would have a lot in common, whereas she was just a—

'Shetland pony.'

Oh, God, I said that out loud!

Her features froze.

'Pardon.'

'I was just—thinking of—breeding Shetland ponies…the miniature ones,' she improvised.

'You ride?'

She knew he did. There was a framed photo of him as a boy: skinny, all scratched legs and thick wild hair, as he sat bareback astride what looked like an excitable grey.

There was still a lot of leg, but nowadays they were muscled columns. She lifted her eyes from the hair-roughened surface she had been staring at, struggling to see the coltish boy with the mop of tangled hair and the cute gaps in his teeth in the man before her, who was the epitome of raw maleness.

'One lesson and I fell off. I didn't get back on.'

'A mistake.'

She shrugged. 'Shetlands are more my size,' she retorted, having almost convinced herself that she wasn't lying. She really was discovering her hidden depths.

'So you're afraid of horses?'

'No, just of heights.'

'Good to know you have your weaknesses.'

She got to her feet, ignoring the gleam of speculation in his dark eyes. Was he wondering how he could exploit her weakness for men who looked like him? Her eyes drifted to his mouth. Men who kissed like him?

Abruptly she veiled her eyes with her lashes and hid behind the wings of her pale hair.

'We have things to discuss,' he said.

She rolled her eyes and shook back her hair. As if he was telling her something she didn't already know. It had actually been a lot better when their conversations had taken place through the intermediary of lawyers.

They did have things to discuss, but it would be a lot more comfortable from her point of view if any discussion took place when he had more clothes on.

She wouldn't have put it past him to have engineered this situation. Actually, she wouldn't put *anything* past him!

'I have plans for this morning,' she said.

His expression was momentarily bemused, as if no one had ever given him the brush-off.

They probably hadn't.

'Plans?'

'I am meeting with Nic, the estate manager, to discuss—'

'Fine. I'll join you.'

Her face fell, alarm widening her eyes and sending her stomach into a sickly dive. He didn't have to say anything or be objectionable. His presence alone would ruin the casual chat over coffee with Nic, who didn't patronise her, or make her feel unqualified, or make her stomach quiver.

'That really won't be—'

She might as well have saved her breath. He was already moving towards the door.

'I can be with you…' A glance at his watch. 'When? Where?' he said casually. 'I'll be there.'

'That r-really isn't—'

He closed down her stuttered protest with a sardonic look. 'What's on the agenda?'

'*Agenda*?' she parroted. 'It's not a board meeting…just a chat and a coffee.'

Although her jangling nerves suggested more coffee would not be a good idea.

He sketched a quick smile and drew a hand down his jaw, drawing her eyes to the dark shadow he hadn't shaved yet.

'Fine. I'll ditch the tie.'

She had *wanted* him to take an interest, and yet now he was the situation seemed more worrying, somehow. But then maybe it was her own antipathy stopping her from viewing this as a good thing, making her suspicious when there was no hidden subtext to read.

She thought there probably was plenty of hidden subtext, but she decided to take a more positive approach. This could be an opportunity to soften Theo's negativity about his inheritance, appeal to his emotional side.

He *must* have had some affection for the place where he had grown up, she reasoned. If she could only reawaken those feelings...

His hand on the wall beside the door, he felt his cynical amusement at the panic written on her face become curiosity as panic faded into resolve.

Catching himself wondering what had put it there, he levered himself off the wall. He was really not interested in her thought processes, or what made her tick...what thoughts were going on in that beautiful head.

He had already admitted that their chemistry—animal attraction, sex, whatever you liked to call it—made total indifference impossible, but he was not about to look beyond the beautiful surface.

Grace arrived at Nic's office before Theo, but only by moments. There was no chance for her to explain to Nic her idea of playing the nostalgia card before Theo walked in, his hair still wet from the shower, his chiselled jaw clean. Along with the chip on his shoulder he seemed to be carrying an almost electrical charge.

Her relief that he was wearing more clothes only lasted a fraction of a second. He was still more handsome than any man had a right to be. From under the sweep of her lashes she took in the details of his outfit: pale blue poplin shirt and grey jeans, a dark belt securing them over narrow hips. He was minus the tie, as promised, and the small vee of deep gold skin at the base of his throat made her stomach muscles quiver.

Before she could gather herself enough to react, Nic was stepping past her, his hand outstretched and a grin pulling his mouth upwards.

'Nico?' Smiling, Theo was moving forward. 'I thought it couldn't be you... The only Nic I know would be as far away from here as he could get!'

Nic clasped the hand extended to him and responded in a burst of warm, fluid Italian before sliding seamlessly back into English.

Grace's mouth opened as she watched the two men exchange a handshake and a masculine thump on the back. Her indignation grew as she watched them—she had been put the other side of the conspiratorial divide.

'I was going to be a rock star, Theo, but things change—people change.'

'Not everything,' Theo said, his face shuttering.

'When Dad got ill I came back…initially to help out.'

'And you stayed?'

Nic nodded and lifted his shoulders in an expressive Latin shrug. '*Si*. And then, after Dad died, Mum moved back to England to be near her twin sister.'

'You weren't tempted to join her?'

'Salvatore asked me to take the job on a permanent basis and, well… I stayed. Got married, had a baby…or actually two.'

Theo, who had stiffened slightly at his father's name, smiled in response to this update. 'Congratulations.' Then his smile faded and his eyes twitched into a straight line above his patrician nose. 'I'm sorry about your father.'

'It was his heart. There had been issues for some time.'

'Sorry, I didn't know.'

Grace thought it was about time to remind them she existed. 'You two know one another? Well, obviously you do,' she said, scrolling through her memory. Had she expressed her opinion on Theo's character a little too robustly to Nic? 'You never said?'

* * *

She'd addressed the comment to Nic, but it was Theo who responded, his lips quirking at the indignation in her voice.

'When you spoke of "Nic" it didn't occur to me that it was Nico...'

He pushed aside the kick of guilt. Far away, it had been easy for him to forget the people whose lives would change when the palazzo and estate changed hands. Being here...

His eyes narrowed. This was not a reason not to divest himself of the past. There was every chance that the new owners would keep Nic and the other staff on after the sale—in fact, he'd make it a condition of sale.

'Theo and I hung out during the holidays when we were kids. I could tell you some stories,' Nic said.

'A threat that scares me,' Theo drawled, a smile in his voice.

It was the first time she had seen him smile for real, and there was enough charm and warmth to tame a tiger and melt an iceberg.

'But remember I also can tell some stories,' he told Nic.

Watching him, she thought he seemed almost human, almost touchable...

She looked away, banished the thought, and

reminded herself that he was hard and callous, and that without her and Marta his father would have died alone.

Lost in her own condemnatory tangle of thoughts, she didn't immediately realise that a chair had been pulled out for her—a courtesy that was Nic's, not Theo's. After a slight hesitation she joined the two men, quickly feeling excluded once more as they began to talk, slipping unconsciously from Italian to English and back.

But not because they were reminiscing. It was all estate business.

Grace had worked hard to get her head around the subject, but a lot of what they were now discussing was way above her.

She was sure that Nic was not deliberately excluding her, but Theo's motives were far less clear-cut, and giving him the benefit of the doubt was a long way off—a distant speck on the horizon.

If Theo was trying to make her feel like an outsider he was succeeding, she decided, resenting the way that he automatically took charge of the discussion and—she had to admit—asked far too knowledgeable questions.

Having slid down in her chair a little, nursing a cup of coffee between her hands, she suddenly pulled herself up, recognising in her muddled thoughts a recurring strand of self-pity.

She was sulking—a fault she thought she had cured.

This wasn't about *them*, it was about *her*, and her lingering sense of inferiority. She might not be as brilliant and beautiful as the rest of her family, and her legs might not be as long, but they worked and so did her brain.

She couldn't blame Nic for being relieved to be talking to someone he didn't have to explain every other sentence to, and Theo was probably enjoying seeing her cold-shouldered out. The way she had been a thousand times before, over the dinner table at home, when everyone got very intellectual or political.

She was playing right into his hands by crawling back in her shell.

'Do you mind running that past me one more time?' she asked. 'I didn't quite…'

Nic flushed and looked guilty. Theo didn't look guilty, but that was no surprise. It was already a given that the man was not capable of feeling guilt.

'Sorry, Grace,' Nic said. 'I was just saying that last year's freak weather affected the olive harvest, but we have great hopes that this year will be a bumper crop.'

'Great—you can put that in your prospectus for potential customers.' She turned to Theo. 'Did Nic tell you we have ambitious plans to expand? Several high-class retail outlets have been showing an interest.'

Theo's brows lifted. 'That detail is good news. As we're selling as a going concern, all details are important.'

A going concern?

That was the first she had heard of it. Her impression had been that the estate would be cut up piecemeal. That getting rid of it quickly was more important than profit. But conscious of Nic, who was looking uncomfortable, she didn't challenge Theo on this.

Instead she responded by simply saying, 'Not *we*.' She blew a feathery wisp of fair hair out of her eyes. '*I'm* not selling.'

Maintaining a smile, even though her cheeks were aching with the effort, she was happy to see her words grated on the intended recipient as she got to her feet.

'If you'll excuse me? I'll leave you both to catch up.'

Spine like steel, she turned and walked out of the room. Indignation took her clear of the building, leaving behind a silence that for one man she knew would be awkward and for the other...

Remembering the glint in his dark eyes, she shook her head. She couldn't figure out what

Theo was thinking—which for her peace of mind was probably for the best.

Despite this silent observation she didn't feel philosophical. She felt frustrated—so frustrated she wanted to scream. Instead she swore softly and fluently under her breath as she walked along the path through the expanse of tall Italian cypress and oak, down the rocky incline towards the beach.

She paused to rest her ankle a few times en route to the horseshoe of sand hemmed in by soft waves that hit the shore with a hiss, dragging fine stones back out as it made its relentless advance and retreat.

The doctor had instructed her to use her ankle and not favour it, but maybe he hadn't meant her to use it quite this much, she decided, wincing as she stepped on a rock half concealed in the sand. The heat was building, but she had been scrupulous about applying her usual factor fifty, so she peeled off her linen shirt and sat down beside it.

She wasn't worried about burning.

CHAPTER FIVE

SHE COULD HAVE yelled aloud now, without anyone coming to rescue her, but the sound of the waves had taken the edge off her jagged feelings as she sat in the sand and focused on the hiss of the waves. Until one wave tickled her toes and she realised that the tide had come in while she had been sitting there.

She got to her feet and slung her folded shirt higher up the sand, then stood hands on hips surveying her surroundings: the turquoise water...the white sand. Despite her claim that she had somewhere else to be, actually Grace didn't. She had grown to love this place with a kind of yearning that went beyond logic, but she couldn't feel it was *hers*. It would take more than words on paper to make that feel real.

She was shocked by how much she *wanted* it to be real...*wanted* to belong to this place. How could Theo want to throw all this away?

The fact remained that she was half owner in

name only, and Theo's appearance had pushed
that knowledge home. He had rejected the palazzo and all it involved, but he *belonged* here
and she didn't. The fact that he didn't want the
place seemed irrelevant—certainly to the people who lived and worked on the estate. His absence and his neglect of his father seemed to
be forgotten and forgiven.

But then, unlike Nic and Marta, they didn't
know he was trying to sell the place out from
under them—well, she assumed they didn't. It
wasn't information she had shared with anyone
else, and she was assuming he wouldn't be taking out a full-page ad any time soon.

No matter what rumours might be floating
around, there was no question that his appearance was viewed with approval—a real Ranieri at the helm. His appearance had changed
everything. Like Nic had, people would automatically look to him now—but she was prepared for it.

It wasn't as if she didn't have experience of
being overlooked. Her family weren't the shy,
retiring type. When they walked into a room
they immediately became the centre of attention, and they all thrived on it.

Whereas Grace genuinely avoided attention.
She was not an 'if you've got it flaunt it' sort of
person. Glancing down at her modest breasts,

she grinned and thought that was just as well, because in some areas she didn't have much to flaunt!

'Non-threatening', her mother had called them when she had complained. At sixteen, Grace had not found this a selling point, but now she recognised that there were plus points—especially on a day like today. She was able to go comfortably braless without worrying about the bounce factor, which was rather nice.

She gave a soft chuckle. While not being resentful about being overlooked, and even though she knew she'd never have the opportunity, it amused her to imagine Theo walking into a room where her family were being their dazzling selves. For once it would be good to see them ignored. Because while her family were dazzling, Theo had that extra undefinable factor that took dazzle to a whole other level.

Her smile faded. Theo would always *belong*—and not just here. She was willing to bet that he had never felt like an outsider anywhere…the person who never really fitted, the one who was always a disappointment.

He had rejected his family, not the other way around.

Grace immediately felt a stab of guilt. Her

family hadn't rejected her…they'd tried to include her, made excuses for her.

We think she might have dyslexia.

Because a dyslexic child was preferable to one who got a B minus in English and maths.

When had she stopped trying?

She frowned at the question that had popped into her head. She liked to leave the past where it was. Besides, there hadn't been a moment… more a gradual realisation that she was never going to do anything good enough to impress her family. So she had embraced her role as the odd one out and consequently been a lot happier.

Why me?

For the thousandth time she asked herself what Salvatore's motivation had been when he'd divided his estate this way. Had he expected her to—?

She gave a despairing sigh as her head dropped to her chest.

When she lifted it, she wriggled the toes of her injured foot in the water, extending her leg to examine it. The bruising was coming out, but the swelling had almost vanished. It seemed possible to walk a little more before she turned back.

It wasn't until she turned that she realised how far she had walked along the shoreline.

This was an area she had not previously explored. She glanced at the unusual rock formation to her right. Curiosity sparked, she began to wade towards the place where the rock protruded from the sea. The fork-like formation brought back Salvatore's voice as he had described a grotto—a magical-sounding cave you could walk into at low tide, with a cavernous crystalline roof that glowed green when the water entered.

She edged along the rock, reaching the point where the rock indented, revealing an entrance, the curved portal of which was exactly the way Salvatore had described it. The water here was only ankle-deep, so she figured there could be no harm in just looking inside. She would explore properly when the tide was out.

Theo did not linger long after Grace had left. The conversation with his old friend had left him feeling restless. Nico belonged to another life—one he had left behind. Yet it had been surprisingly easy to pick up the threads of their shared experiences as though the intervening years had not existed.

But it wasn't this that occupied his thoughts… it was the look of hurt he had seen in Grace's blue eyes when his gaze had drifted her way.

Why should it bother him?

He didn't want her to feel wanted. The whole idea was to isolate her, make her life uncomfortable.

Her expression reminded him of a kid at school—the one who had never fitted in. The one who had been bullied until Theo had made it known he was under this protection.

Her look had made Theo feel as if he was one of the bullies.

Annoyed by his irrational response, he took the cliff path back to the house. He needed to contact his office. Frustration rushed over him. He needed not to be here. He needed not to have old wounds reopened.

At first he thought it was a bird that he could hear, and then he realised it was a phone ringing. After a moment he located the sound to a small, indeterminate pile of clothing on the beach. Rather than following the pathway down, he scaled the cliff, muscle memory kicking in as he found the footholds he remembered from his youth.

As he approached the pile the phone began to ring again, beneath the haphazardly discarded pair of sandals and a white linen shirt. Grace's. He remembered it being open and baggy. Without it her fair skin would burn.

He felt a deep flutter in his belly as he grabbed the shirt almost angrily. Without thinking, he lifted it to his face, inhaling the fragrance clinging to the fabric before he realised what he was doing.

With a curse, he dropped it and scanned the sand and the sea beyond. There was no sign of its sweet-smelling owner. Then his narrowed eyes caught the darker indentations in the sand near the water line. There might have been other footsteps, but the tide was coming in fast.

The phone started ringing again, shrill and insistent, but this time it cut off quickly and a moment later it pinged.

As he picked it up, he could see the words.

Assuming you have seen the scurrilous article...?

He read the name of a tabloid that specialised in the scurrilous.

If you'd planned to come to your sister's awards ceremony next week maybe rethink. This is her night...

The rest of the message was hidden, fading from the screen as Theo, his expression thoughtful, stared at the blank screen.

He had not seen the article referenced, but the name of the tabloid made it hard not to guess the theme: *Young nurse left a fortune by elderly patient.*

His jaw tightened as he swore under his breath. The timing and the leak had Rollo's fingerprints all over.

He could only assume that planting the story was Rollo's idea of helping the cause—showing initiative.

He scored a line in the sand with his foot... a line that Rollo wouldn't have recognised if he'd fallen over it.

If the guy had not gone off-piste this way... if he had run it past him—

Theo blinked, an expression of shock spreading across his lean face as it hit him. If Rollo had run the idea past him twenty-four hours ago he would have likely told him to go ahead.

The furrow in his brow deepened as he realised that during that time his plans had shifted and realigned in his head in a way he wasn't comfortable with. It was as inexplicable as the prickle of guilt that he was experiencing.

He replayed the message in his head, which he presumed must have come from one of Grace's family members. Unless there was a supportive section in the latter portion of the text it would seem that Grace wasn't about to receive any tea and sympathy from her nearest and dearest. Which could mean she was a repeat offender, who had embarrassed them previously, or they were heartless bastards.

Or none of the above, he added, aware that he was guilty of the sort of speculation he usually frowned on.

Either way, it would seem she didn't have a support network to fall back on—which should have made him feel happier than it actually did.

He wandered towards the place where he had spotted the footprints, but they were already being sucked into the swirls of water before vanishing like—*like she had vanished.*

He froze, belatedly aware of where he was standing.

A moment later he was not standing. He had kicked off his trainers and was wading into the water. It felt like tortuously slow progress, and Theo felt a surge of relief when he was able to kick away from the bottom and swim.

Head down, in seconds he'd made it through the iconic arch and surfaced, treading water, thinking perhaps his reaction had been an instinct too far. He searched the cavernous cathedral-like interior that appeared to be lit by a deep, subterranean green reflected off the water.

Almost immediately he saw her, sitting like some sort of stranded mermaid—albeit with pale, slender legs—on a stone shelf.

A stranded mermaid in cut-offs and a cling-ing vest top.

His relief morphed into anger—the logic-cancelling variety.

Cleaving through the water with a few strong strokes, he brought himself up to her side and floated there, treading water.

Grace blinked at the flood of angry, fluid Ital-ian—which, despite her recent lessons, was ut-terly incomprehensible. The emotion behind the flow of words from the dark-haired fig-ure floating below her, however, did not need translation.

'Hello.'

It sounded so stupid she began to laugh, the tension and fear of the last few minutes evapo-rating into a weird euphoria.

The speed with which the water had risen when she had emerged from her awed contem-plation of the cave had shocked her, but she hadn't panicked. Instead she had escaped the tug of water that was driving her deeper into the cave by dragging herself up onto a rocky ledge that ran along the side. Of course it had quickly become clear that she'd have been bet-ter off panicking and swimming out straight away, hoping for the best, before the swirling water got scarily high.

Now the strong surge of the current made it unlikely she'd even make it through the arch into the open sea.

When Theo had appeared she had almost decided that her best hope—her only hope—would be to swim for it before the opening was totally covered by the incoming tide.

'You think this is funny?'

She totally appreciated his outrage. She also appreciated, even at a moment like this, how incredible he looked. His dark hair was clinging to his skull, to the perfect bones of his perfect face, and the sybaritic angles and planes were defined against his wet, olive-toned skin.

'Not at all,' she soothed.

He didn't seem soothed. He looked hotly furious.

'You—'

She could almost see him bite his tongue, and his next words were spaced evenly and enunciated with elaborate calm.

'Can you swim?'

'Of course I can swim.' Otherwise she'd be…well, dead. 'I'm not a great swimmer, but I don't sink—not straight away,' she admitted.

Theo cleared his throat and crafted his civilised response with the utmost difficulty. There would be plenty of time to tell her what he thought of her later. The present problem was what he needed to focus on.

'Right, you do what you can. Let's get out of here.'

He glanced over his shoulder towards the exit that had grown even smaller while he had wasted precious seconds noticing how her small, pointed breasts with their thrusting nipples looked under the clinging wet fabric.

As if he was judging a wet tee shirt competition.

Silently deriding himself for his distraction, he urged her with an imperative gesture to join him.

Hands pressed to the rocky surface, about to lower herself back into the salty water, she paused. 'Just to check…you can swim quite well?'

She knew it was a silly question even as she voiced it. He would do everything well. He was not a man who screamed mediocrity.

Normally perfect people irritated her, but on this occasion his perfection was comforting.

Theo angled her a look through the drops of water trembling on his dark lashes. '*Very* well,' he said, with no display of false modesty, reaching up a hand to support her as she dropped down.

She was conscious as she did so that she was

shaking, fine tremors that rippled through her entire body.

'Right, stay close.'

'I will—' she began, then choked as salty water blocked her airway and she spluttered unattractively.

What is wrong with me? Worrying about looking attractive when I'm about to drown?

But she wasn't. That soon became clear. Theo had not exaggerated his claim to swim very well, though even he struggled to get them both safely through the gap, where their heads were scarily close to the rocky arch of their exit. He literally dragged her out at one point, having flipped her over onto her back, with one iron arm strapped around her middle, and kicked hard before the escape route closed.

'You can open your eyes now,' said a voice very close to her ear.

Grace did, and blinked, dazzled, as she stared up into the blue sky overhead—a blue sky she had not allowed herself to think she'd ever see again.

She turned her head and saw the dark face of her rescuer.

'Thank you.'

Theo found the urge to throttle her fading as those blue eyes met his, glowing with gratitude.

'You didn't panic. Well done.'

'Oh, God, don't be nice to me or I'll start crying.'

'You already are.'

'You are so pedantic,' she sniffed—before a wave washed over her head, leaving her spluttering.

'I'd love to hang around here chatting, but we need to move or the tide will take us back into the grotto.'

Grace realised that the entrance was now totally covered in water. She nodded. But the shore looked a long way off.

'Just do what you can and I'll do the rest,' he said, obviously seeing her fearful look.

She nodded again and set her chin.

It seemed a long time later when he said, 'You can stand up now.'

'Easy for you to say,' she mumbled, stretching down to feel the sandy floor, bobbing on one leg to keep her head above the water.

Watching her pale hair streaming around her face like exotic strands of seaweed, as she breathlessly bounced and quite incredibly joked, Theo felt something nameless shift inside him.

She would have been entitled to milk the drama, but here she was cracking jokes. Whatever else she was, she was no coward. Nor, for that matter, a drama queen.

Grace's legs were shaking as, arms outstretched, she strode towards the strip of sand. There was a lot less of it than there had been the last time she'd seen it.

When she got knee high in the water she stood there, her chest lifting with the laboured breaths that sucked in the muscles of her belly, and pushed both shaking hands over her dripping hair, squeezing the water out of the ends.

She turned her head and saw Theo was watching her. His stare made her painfully conscious that her clothes were clinging like a second skin. She fought the urge to wrap her arms around herself and instead returned his stare steadily.

She could hardly come over all Victorian virgin and tell him to avert his eyes. The man had just saved her life and, while the drenched clothes were revealing, they were less so than a bikini. Besides, he was hardly going to be overcome with lust.

Maybe that's your problem?

Almost stumbling as she caught herself in

the insane thought that she *wanted* him to lust after her, she threw herself onto the sand.

Theo watched as she took a couple of steps before falling full-length onto the sand, arms and legs outstretched. For a split second he thought she'd collapsed. And then she turned her head to reveal a cheek coated with sand and began to move her supple limbs.

'A sand angel!' she cried, flipping over and repeating the process on her back, her laughing face turned to the sky.

'How much salt water did you swallow?' he asked, amused despite himself.

Her joy was contagious.

She pulled herself into a sitting position, sand-coated knees drawn up to her chin, and started to dust off the wet sand that adhered to her face, only managing to deposit more from her sand-encrusted hands.

'I'm celebrating being alive,' she said, conscious as she stared up at the impossibly tall man standing there that she must have looked… did still look…ridiculous.

No man should be able to look both authoritative and breathtakingly handsome in soggy clothes, with water literally dripping off his lean body, but Theo managed the impossible.

She thought despairingly that he looked as sexy as a dark fallen angel…or even Lucifer himself.

'I was being spontaneous.'

She lowered her eyes and gave a self-conscious half-shrug before reaching for her discarded shirt. The action dislodged her phone from its resting place, and it fell to the sand a couple of feet away. She took a couple of squelchy steps and picked it up, nursing it against her chest as she turned to face him and found his eyes on her, the expression in their dark depths impenetrable.

To fill the lengthening uncomfortable silence and drown out the thundering sound of her heartbeat, Grace rushed into speech.

'Lucky I left it here or it would have been ruined.'

She winced at the chirpy sound of her own voice, but felt a rush of relief when he veiled his eyes.

In Theo's experience, people who always looked on the bright side, even when there wasn't one, fell into two camps: the unintelligent and the irritating.

The former he could forgive. The latter…

Grace was not unintelligent, and despite this he found himself fighting off a smile.

'Oh, yes, that shows great foresight,' he

drawled. 'If you're going to drown yourself, the number one thing to remember is to protect your mobile devices.'

Grace scowled, but clearly her heart wasn't in it as she fixed him with her big blue stare.

'I know you probably don't want to make a big thing of it, but you did save my life.'

'By all means make a big thing of it,' encouraged Theo, who usually very much disliked the idea of gushing gratitude. 'I'm gutted you're not telling me I'm your hero.'

'I'm grateful, but let's not go overboard...' She paused, her soft lips quivering slightly, as she brushed more of the drying sand from her upper arms.

Her brush with death was clearly too recent for her to keep up the facade of flippancy. Despite the sun that was beating down, he could see that her skin beneath the layer of sand was marbled with goosebumps.

'Can you walk?' he asked, his brusqueness disguising an inconvenient stab of concern as he looked down at her.

Utterly mortified by the fact that she must be coming across like some swooning Victorian maiden in a melodrama, who fell at the hero's feet in every scene, Grace lifted her chin.

'Of course I can walk,' she retorted coolly,

proving the fact by taking a firm step away from him—too firm for her ankle, but she kept the wince inside.

Her action hadn't taken her clear of his personal raw male, mind-numbing zone, but it was an improvement.

'I don't make a habit of—'

Coming across as a total incapable fool.

She paused to tuck her hair behind her ears in a businesslike fashion. 'Obviously I am very grateful…'

'But you don't want to be?'

'This is very embarrassing for me!' she flung, responding angrily to the mockery in his face. 'This is not me. I'm not a person who needs rescuing. I'm the person who makes other people feel safe.'

Deep frustration pushed the words from her lips…words which were followed by taut silence.

'Is that what you did for my—for Salvatore?'

The hands clenched at her sides relaxed as she shot a questioning glance up at him, but her attempt to read his expression was frustrated by his shuttered expression.

'I hope so. I think I did.'

'Were you there when…?' The question seemed to come almost against his will.

'He wasn't alone.' She offered the information quietly. 'Marta and I were both there with him when he slipped away.'

Theo said nothing as he stood there, his feelings hidden behind an impassive mask. He felt the pain like an exposed nerve as a layer of his emotional isolation was stripped away.

He told himself that it was because of this place he hated…this place his father had loved.

'He really is dead.'

He'd spoken as though the reality had just hit him, and Grace felt an unwilling surge of empathy.

'I'm not, though…thanks to you.'

He looked down as if he had forgotten she was there. 'We need to get you back up to the palazzo.'

She talked tough but she looked so fragile, he thought. So damned vulnerable standing there.

He wanted—wanted…

Instead of analysing what he wanted he growled out, '*Dio*, but you need a keeper.'

She stuck her chin out. 'I don't need to be *got* anywhere. I'm not a parcel. I am more than capable of taking myself. I know they say that if you save someone's life it's your responsibility

KIM LAWRENCE 109

for ever, but don't take it too literally—I really don't make a habit of needing rescuing.'

It seemed a point worth emphasising, and she already had an entire family who would run her life if she allowed them to.

He gave a faint sardonic smile. 'Do they say that?'

She shrugged. 'I might have got that wrong,' she admitted.

'So you have to save my life now?'

His sardonic smile deepened into a wry grin and she tossed him a look that suggested she might leave him to his fate if the roles were reversed.

'I am assuming you were not one of those little girls who fantasised about being rescued by a handsome prince.'

She lifted her eyebrows as she shrugged on the oversized shirt, which chafed against the sand on her skin but at least offered some protection from the midday sun.

'*Handsome!* My, you do think a lot of yourself,' she came back. But she was thinking, *And not without good cause.*

Not that 'handsome' covered what he was, she decided, as her eyes moved with helpless fascination over the strong, powerful contours of his face before sliding lower over his lean body. A shudder rippled through her body as she remembered the tensile strength of the hard body that had supported her, that had driven them both through the water with sleek efficiency.

'Lucky you're around to keep my ego in check.'

She snorted. It seemed to her that his bullet-proof vest ego would survive any natural disaster and several manmade ones.

'My sister and I were encouraged to think of ourselves as the ones who should be doing the rescuing.'

He fell into step beside her as she moved towards the path, the rocks they trod on worn smooth from years of use.

'So you have a sister?' he said casually, although he already knew the answer from that brief file he had scanned.

She nodded. 'A sister and two brothers.'

She started, as the phone she was clutching beeped. She glanced at the screen automatically and then paused, gnawing down on her full lower lip as she threw out a hurried, 'Sorry, I should check…'

There were three messages and a heap of missed calls.

Scanning the first message, she felt her heart

take a lurching journey to her feet. Apparently a tabloid had run the story of her inheritance, and had produced a piece that was a mix of truth, lies and smutty innuendo.

Her parents were asking her, under the circumstances, not to come to an awards ceremony for her sister the next week. Her presence would be 'a distraction'.

Grace correctly translated that as an *embarrassment*. But you could see their point.

Things did not get better.

The second message said that a hastily called family conference had decided it would be best for her to sell up and make a sizeable donation to charity with the proceeds, to mitigate the bad publicity. In other words she was not to fight the fact she had been found guilty in the court of public opinion.

The last message told her not to worry—they had put the case in the hands of Uncle Charlie, known to the world as Sir Charles Taverner KC, a lawyer who litigated for the great, the good and the famous. He would sort it all out for her.

They would all be pleased to see her, of course but actually it might be better for her to stay where she was, sit tight until things had died down, because two news channels had already picked up the story and dug out a picture of her in a bikini from somewhere…

Oh, well, a *bikini*… That really made her a scarlet woman.

A one-line postscript telling her that maybe she should beef up her security made her glance over her shoulder nervously.

Theo watched her scroll through the messages, her face partially shielded by the wings of her lint-pale wet hair.

But even without being able to see the play of emotion across her face he could read her body language, the tension in her shoulders, and the white knuckles on her free hand made it clear that what she was reading was not good news.

'A problem?' he asked.

She compressed her lips over a snarled response. 'Not one that would interest you,' she replied tightly—and then thought it probably would, as seeing her reputation trashed in the tabloid press would only…

What…?

Would it help him?

She had no idea, but she knew that the idea of her life being trawled through made her feel sick, even though it would make pretty boring reading.

'If you're contacted by a lawyer claiming to work for me, don't believe him,' she told him grimly. 'He doesn't speak for me.'

Her parents, who had been unusually hands-off so far, had clearly reverted to type in response to the tabloid threat to the family name. They were staging a takeover bid.

In the past she had often given in for a quiet life, saving her resistance for the times when it really mattered to her.

This mattered to her.

'Is that likely?' he asked.

'Oh, yes,' she replied grimly, gently swatting away a bee disturbed when she'd brushed against the wild herbs growing along the pathway.

'This person is not a lawyer?'

Her eyes widened as she responded bitterly. 'He's a very *expensive* lawyer, but not *my* lawyer. He's my parents' best friend and my godfather. However, even though I have no doubt he'll say things you want to hear, he does not speak for me.'

'So you intend to say things I do not want to hear?'

'Yes…that is, no. I'm not selling.'

She threw him a sideways look, expecting him to react, but he didn't.

His expression was—

She frowned, unable to read his expression…

CHAPTER SIX

'YOU'RE NOT ON good terms with your family? Maybe it's time to cut your losses and dump them.'

His words broke into the mental list of home truths she wanted to deliver at the next family meeting.

She stared at him.

'Cut my losses?' she echoed. 'This is not a financial deal—this is my family!'

He shrugged. 'Therefore a million times more toxic.'

'You don't cut yourself off from your family just because they're impossible sometimes. Families disagree, but they— I *love* my family,' she gritted out through clenched teeth, before giving a little laugh.

He frowned at her laugh, and as she scanned his beautiful, austere, *implacable* face, she could see that he hadn't understood a word she had said.

'If I let them, my family would run my life. They would…*suffocate* me. They are beautiful, talented, and not at all like me. They're like you,' she added, flicking a critical look up at his lean face before wondering why she was telling him this, when she knew there was zero chance of him getting it.

'I'm assuming that is not a compliment,' he said.

Grace had started walking as they spoke, and as they reached the lower tier of the manicured terraces he noticed she was limping.

'It seems to me sentimental and self-destructive to maintain contact with people who make you unhappy, who manipulate you, manipulate the truth…'

'I can't believe that Salvatore manipulated you!' she exclaimed, without thinking.

He froze, and so did his expression. 'We are not talking about my family. We are talking about yours.'

The sardonic lift of her feathery brow made him grind his teeth, but it was the knowing sympathy in her blue eyes that sent his temper surging into the red zone.

'Maybe,' she said quietly, 'we should not talk at all.'

She slung the words over her shoulder as she

began to trudge ahead—no, not trudge, *limp*, he corrected, watching her through narrowed eyes.

After a moment of watching her, he gave a sigh.

It took him seconds to overtake her.

'You have hurt your foot again?' he accused.

Grace, her face set, attempted to sidestep around him.

He mirrored her.

Teeth gritted, she stopped.

As much as she would have liked to try, he wasn't the sort of person you could nudge out of the way or walk through.

'No, the other one.' She knew she must sound like some sort of accident-prone idiot. 'It's nothing, really… Just sand in my sandal and it's rubbing.'

She lifted the painful foot off the ground.

He sighed and looked exasperated and bored at the same time. 'Then getting the sand out would seem like a solution.'

Childishly, she wanted to refuse. But his suggestion, even if it was couched as an order, made common sense.

'You don't have to wait,' she said as she lowered herself onto a large smooth rock, taking care not to crush the alpine plant with its spikes of orange flowers that was crawling over it. 'I'll catch you up.'

She added a silent postscript—*Not!*

She was curling up her leg to loosen the buckle across her foot when he dropped into a casual squat beside her. She felt a flare of alarm as his dark face came level with her own and thought, *What do you not understand about 'I'll catch you up'?*

How, she wondered, casting him a look through her lashes, could anyone look so elegant when they had to be squelching?

After a moment she reacted to his imperative gesture and his look of impatience and extended her foot, reluctance etched into her face and the action.

She sat immobile, breathing shallowly as he took the sandal by the heel and drew it over her narrow foot. Dropping it, he held her foot, turning it lightly from side to side, seeing the red inflamed area under the crusting of damp and drying sand.

The clicking sound of his tongue suggested to Grace that he thought she had done it on purpose, just to irritate him, but nothing could have been more gentle or clinical than his touch as he brushed the sand away, exposing a small blister below the protrusion of her ankle and a wider reddened area on the pale blue veined skin.

His job was done, but he didn't release her foot, and neither did Grace withdraw it. She was experiencing a strange, not-quite-there, drugged dreamy sensation as his long square-tipped fingers moved over the delicate bones of her foot almost as though he was memorising them.

Grace's breath came in short, shallow, staccato gasps. She was unable to see his face so she stared at the top of his dark head. The sun was already starting to dry the glossy raven strands, but she felt sure that had she sunk her hands into the abundant growth it would have been wet against his scalp.

She wouldn't, obviously.

Her flexing fingertips didn't seem to hear the message. She had actually half extended her hand when he dropped her foot abruptly and sank back on his heels, grabbing her sandal and handing it to her.

As if released from a spell, Grace started to breathe again, the heat that had expanded in her belly putting colour in her pale cheeks.

She snatched the sandal from his hand, reacting to some inbuilt protective instinct and taking care not to make contact with his fingers.

'I have some plasters in my room…fast healing for blisters,' she babbled inanely as she thrust her foot back into her sandal. And then, in case he thought she was asking him to help, she added far too brightly, 'I'm quite a dab hand with plasters…medical training and all…'

She was addressing her flow of words to her feet and not the man beside her.

She began to struggle to her feet, pretending she had not seen the hand extended to her, which was quickly dropped as its owner stood back to watch her.

Stubborn, hard-headed little witch.

'I hope you are not expecting me to carry you?' he said.

His hooded gaze slid down her slim, supple curves, moulded by saturated clothing, and he made the mistake of allowing the memory of how she had felt warm and soft in his arms to surface and taunt him.

Seven and a half stone wet and encrusted with sand… An image formed in his head of removing not just the sand on her slender foot but from her entire body…the smooth supple expanses and the secret crevices.

He dropped his hand and rose abruptly to his feet. He knew there was no water available that would cool the heat that hardened his body.

'I think I'll manage,' she said, addressing her dry retort to the left side of shoulder.

But somehow she encountered his eyes, dark and—

The expression in them and the damped-down heat in their darkness made her stomach muscles quiver violently.

It was not one of the search parties that Marta had sent out that found them but Marta herself, and she listened to the story of the grotto delivered by Theo with an expression of horror on her face.

Grace stood passively listening to the interchange and shot him a fulminating glare. He might have played down his own heroism, but he had definitely played up her helplessness and stupidity.

The older woman looked white with shock as she took Grace's arm, and Grace experienced a spasm of guilt.

'Oh—you must be—let me…'

'I'm fine,' Grace insisted, but was not actually believed by any of the four members of the house staff who had materialised and were now listening to her protests.

Story of my life.

By the time she had been ushered tenderly into the palazzo, as though she was made of glass, through the double doors that led to the kitchen and its associated utility rooms, Theo had vanished.

She envied and resented his vanishing act.

Theo had taken the call out of idle curiosity, he told himself. The man had been urbane, witty and warm—presumably to make him, the recipient of his honeyed tone, lower his defences before he got to the actual subject of his call.

'A lovely girl, little Grace… And I have to own to a personal interest here. She's actually my favourite goddaughter, but stubborn…you have to know how to handle her—'

Theo, without knowing why, cut across this flow of confidences. 'No.'

'I beg your pardon?'

'I said, no. Has Grace appointed you as her spokesperson? Do you speak on her behalf?'

'Not exactly. But her family… The thing is, dear chap, we both want the same thing here. And if we were to combine…'

Taking exception to the conspiratorial tone, Theo stiffened. 'So that's a no. I have to say, Sir Charles, I find your attitude a tad…*unprofessional*.'

There was an audible indignant inhalation on the other end of the phone, but also, when he responded, Theo noted a defensive undertone to his response that hadn't been there previously.

'We— Her family— I am looking out for Grace's interests.'

'You have the advantage,' said Theo. 'I do not know Grace. But what I have seen of her so far does not suggest to me that she needs anyone to look after her interests. She is a remarkably capable woman.'

If accident-prone and bloody infuriating, he tacked on silently.

'Well, yes, of course. But—'

'Sorry, but I have another call. Feel free to contact my assistant at any time.'

His phone rang almost immediately.

It was his assistant, which made him smile.

'I know you're going to be angry and yell…'

'I never yell.'

'You yell quietly,' she retorted.

'Loren…?'

'All right. Look, I'm sorry… I know you asked me to clear your schedule, and I did. Except I forgot something. And I know it's just a courtesy, but you cancelled your game the last few times, and—'

'Leonard! *Damn!*'

Leonard Morris, who had refused a knighthood, was a legend. Theo had conned his way into his office when he was a kid, with big ideas and not much of a clue, and the other man had had his security team throw him out.

Theo had gone back the next day, when Leonard had not given him a job, or advice, but he hadn't thrown him out either. Instead he had offered to play him at chess. Leonard had won and Theo had learnt.

He thought that he had learnt more from their chess games and post-game analysis than he would have at the best university.

Their games had since become a bi-monthly event. Once it had been Leonard who had made time for him. Since Leonard's retirement it had been Theo who made time for Leonard.

It wasn't a good deed. He found the older man's mind as sharp as ever, and fascinating, and hoped that one day, if he was lucky, he might be in Leonard's position.

'Don't cancel.'

The trip would give him an opportunity to tell Rollo in person just how far he had overstepped the mark with that press leak.

The new file he had submitted still lay unopened on his laptop. Theo did not delve too deeply into the reason for his lack of urgency in opening it. Perhaps he liked the idea that life still offered some surprises, he mused, thinking of cobalt blue eyes.

Theo strolled into the library. 'Are you ready?'

Grace dropped the book she had picked up

and all the kinks that had vanished from her spine returned, along with the beginnings of a headache.

'I thought you'd left.'

But silently and without an explanation here he was, looking...

Her eyes made a veiled sweep of his tall frame, from his feet to his glossy dark head.

He was not dressed for the office, more the beach, in khaki swimming shorts and a black tee shirt that exposed his muscular biceps.

Her sensitive stomach muscles quivered.

She smiled and dismissed the physical response. Eye candy, she told herself dismissively, and immediately experienced an inner cringe moment. It was a lazy analogy, and maybe showed the level of chaos he created in her head.

Grace knew that there was a lot more to the man than the body of a Greek god.

'I'm back. Did you miss me?'

She wanted to say, *I barely noticed*, but she was basically an honest person.

Instead she snorted, but didn't quite meet his eyes. 'It has been quiet and peaceful. Ready for what?' she added, thinking, *I knew it was too good to be true*.

He produced a megawatt smile, all perfect

teeth and hidden meaning. 'Getting back on the horse.'

'I don't ride.'

'The grotto.'

She tensed, images of the event flashing through her head. 'What about it?'

'You're scared, and there is no shame in that.'

Her chin went up, and then up a little more, because he was smiling. 'I'm *not* scared.'

'I've had a tedious flight—a drunk decided he wanted to exit at thirty thousand feet. This is what you get for being conscious of your carbon footprint. First class is overrated when compared to a private jet. But let's not go there. I was going to go for a swim to loosen up, and I thought of my last swim…'

His expression was impassive, the words innocuous, but his honey-toned delivery made her skin prickle—and not with suspicion.

The fact was she *had* been relieved when he had vanished with no word, no explanation—so typical of his arrogance!

It had been the not knowing if or when he would return that had bothered her…not his absence. The fact she hadn't been able to let her defences down completely. Missing him would be like missing the absence of a pain in the rear.

But had things felt a little flat with him not around?

She pushed away the laughable idea. She liked a quiet life and it had been very quiet—and peaceful. Twenty-four hours without being constantly on edge.

Boring?

She ignored the silent intervention in her head.

'Enjoy your swim,' she said flashing him a brilliantly insincere smile.

'So have you resisted the scene of the crime?'

'I have been to the beach several times and stayed in the shallows.'

'You need to face your fears.'

'I really don't need advice from you. If I want my head examined, my brother is a psychiatrist.'

'Interesting family...'

He'd know just how interesting, he assumed, when he got around to reading Rollo's file, which he had been promised held some 'juicy stuff'. The man's ebullient confidence seemed undimmed by his tongue-lashing from Theo.

Though Theo had not immediately made the connection, he now realised that he'd once met Grace's sister. She had seemed to him at the time brittle and driven—which were no bad things—but also a little insecure...the sort of insecure that made her show off.

In retrospect, he could feel more sympathy for her—at the time he'd just been irritated when she'd spoken over people and missed every social cue.

It had to be hard for any woman, having a sister like Grace, who was not only beautiful, but natural, with a quirky charm and smartness that couldn't be learnt.

'Fascinating,' Grace said waspishly, clearly not focusing on her inner charm.

'Look, the offer stands,' he told her. 'Come and explore the grotto and it won't be the scary place it has become in your head. It's low tide and perfectly safe. We can wade in and walk out—job done.'

'Is this a trick? Why are you being so nice?'

'Not nice…'

His mind slid back to yesterday's chess game. He had lost, and when he'd said ruefully he wasn't sure why, Leonard had asked him if he actually wanted to know.

Amused, Theo had said yes. 'I am not afraid of a hard truth,' he had joked.

'You have a tendency to take a fixed position before examining the evidence,' Leonard had said. 'That inflexibility, it makes you vulnerable, Theo. You miss opportunities.'

He knew the old man could not see into his head, but it sometimes seemed awfully like it.

He was not about to change his mind, but he was also not about to prejudge Grace. He would get to know her.

'It won't be deep?' she asked.

He shrugged off his light-hearted attitude. 'I have been afraid of things in my life. Believe me, it is better to face your devils and laugh at them.'

Half an hour later Grace found herself standing on the beach, trembling as though the temperature was sub-zero and not a balmy twenty-three. She had no idea why, but knew it must have seemed like a good idea at the time.

She welcomed the distraction when Theo stripped off his top, revealing the slabbed perfection of his flat belly and the definition of his bronzed chest.

'The first step is always the hardest,' he said.

'I'm not scared.'

'I know.'

She was gripping his hand and she didn't really know how or why. The ankle-deep ripples were innocuous and warm against her bare skin. Then the water reached above her ankles and her stomach muscles clenched.

'Nice swimsuit.'

It was plain black, high on the leg and scooped at the back and front, quite low, but secure. She was not afraid of anything falling out because she didn't have that much there. If she had, his comment would have made her very nervous. As it was, it just provided a useful distraction.

'You're doing great.'

She smiled and stopped looking at her feet. 'I am... I really am!' she agreed fervently, and then, as their eyes clashed, she added a soft, 'Thanks for this.'

She didn't care if he had an ulterior motive. He was doing her a massive favour, and she had never been one to hold a grudge.

She released his hand as they entered the grotto.

'It is so beautiful...' she breathed, turning full circle as she gazed around the echoey chamber. The nightmare images in her head were losing their grip...she could almost hear them receding into the distance. 'It feels I should whisper—like in a church.'

'So, not scary?' he asked, watching the look of wonder on her face as she tilted her head back and spun around, her silver-blonde hair spilling down her back.

He felt the years peel away as he saw the place fresh through her eyes, remembered how it had used to feel this way to him once, before everything had become poisoned in his head.

'No, just beautiful...*awesome*.' She took a deep breath and smiled up at him sunnily. 'You saved me twice.'

The warmth and uncomplicated gratitude in her face as she smiled into his face took his breath away.

She didn't appear to register his sharp intake of breath as, with a slight furrow in her brow, she looked around the space, struggling to get her bearings. He knew all her recollections would be through the filter of fear.

'I sat up there?' Her eye lifted to the ledge where she had sought refuge.

It was a long way up.

'The tide here is so—' She stopped as her eyes went fearfully to the arched stone entrance.

'We are quite safe.'

She nodded and instinctively moved in closer to his side. 'It all looks so different.'

And the outcome, she realised, could have been very different indeed.

'I am grateful, you know—I'm very glad you were here and you didn't walk away.'

His expression froze. 'Is that who you think I am? Someone who walks away?'

Aware she had struck a nerve, and surprised by it, she responded evenly. 'I don't know you well enough to make any judgement. I don't know who you are. But I do know for *sure*,' she emphasised, 'that without you I would not be here. That's all I'm trying to say. I'm not normally so reckless.'

Some of the stiffness left his face.

'This was my playground when I was a child,' he said. His expansive gesture took in the incredible glittering ceiling above their head. 'You wouldn't be the first person to be caught out by the tides. There was a camera crew in the eighties, apparently, that barely escaped. They lost a fortune's worth of photographic gear, so the story goes. Nature is not something that adapts to you—you have to do the adapting.'

She nodded, looking up at him and wondering if she was seeing the real Theo, before lowering her eyes, but not her defences. That *would* be reckless. Seeing something she wanted to see, something that wasn't there, was a trap she was not about to blunder into.

'It was stupid…careless of me,' she said.

And it would be even more stupid to believe that there was more to this man than met the eye—that she had some sort of unique insight. Women had been thinking they would be the one who saw the good in a bad boy—they would be the one to reform him—from time immemorial.

'Don't beat yourself up,' he told her.

Good advice, she thought.

'I won't.' A wave lapped at her feet and she shivered. 'Should we be going back?' she asked nervously.

'You're safe with me.'

The crazy thing was, she realised, replaying his words in her head, she believed it. At that moment he made her feel safe—and yet he was the most dangerous man she had ever met.

Like the man himself, her feelings were totally contradictory.

They walked back to the beach in silence—not comfortable, but not innately confrontational either. For once he wasn't goading her. He seemed lost in his own thoughts.

Standing on the beach, she felt unease return. He was not staring, but she was suddenly conscious that she was in a swimsuit. She replaced her oversized sunglasses on her nose. A tent to hide behind would have been nice, but they were at least something.

'Perhaps we should talk,' he said.

She tensed. The charm offensive seemed to be over. 'About what?'

'Our situation. This doesn't have to be a war of attrition, you know.'

She stared at him warily and ran a hand over the low ponytail that confined her silvery hair.

'Doesn't it?'

'There has to be some middle ground,' he began, feeling his way.

He was not surprised she looked confused. He wasn't even sure himself what he was suggesting. In his head, compromise had always equated with weakness.

Was he thinking about a compromise?

Had he gone soft? Or was he reacting to the tug of those blue eyes now hidden behind the dark lenses? Or was he simply asking himself the wrong questions?

He felt a surge of self-irritation. This wasn't complicated. It was sex. The fact was he had never wanted a woman the way he wanted Grace Stewart. The hunger was just eating him up. And it wasn't just sex he needed—which had been his first assumption—it was her. A fact that had been brought home to him when he'd bumped into an ex-lover at the airport and found himself refusing her offer to spend the night with him.

'I belonged here once,' he said, his gaze sweeping over the panorama, the scene soaking into him, awakening memories that were not all bad.

Or possibly he had started seeing the place through Grace's eyes…her rose-tinted spectacles.

He had no idea if it was feasible, sharing this place with her, but he did know he wanted to share a bed with her. For the sake of his sanity, that was non-negotiable. The sexual charge between them was tangible, but she seemed reluctant to acknowledge it—an attitude that seemed strange to him in someone who seemed so up-front in every other way.

'When did that change?' she asked.

His dark eyes levelled on her face, and after a tense second stretched into a minute he shrugged and said abruptly, 'My mother died.'

Her blue eyes shone with compassion. 'How old were you?'

'Thirteen.'

Grace took a deep breath and came to a decision. A person had to eat, and it would be good to break the deadlock. Also, she was now immune—or very nearly immune—to his smile.

'All right.'

The glitter in his eyes made her stomach dip, but a moment later it was gone as he nodded casually.

'Later, then.'

Was this some sort of trap? she wondered,

watching him stride away, excitement quivering through her. If so, it was a trap she had jumped into blindly. But it was so far out of her comfort zone that Mars would have felt safer and more familiar than the path she was walking.

Just dinner, cautioned a voice in her head. And, being a realist, Grace listened to it.

CHAPTER SEVEN

GRACE WAS FIVE-THREE, and she wore heels whenever the opportunity arose.

However, although her ankle was better, it was not *that* much better, and it was deeply frustrating to have that option taken off the table when she was about to share a table—was that the right phrase?—with a man who made her feel like a hobbit.

She had selected, quite accidentally, her sexiest dress. A short, silky teal shift with a slight gather and a side tie at the waist, designed to hide any thickening around the waist area. She cinched in the defining sash absently, without looking at her reflection.

Grace had no added inches to disguise—she would have actually welcomed a few extra pounds—but when it came to clothes and her appearance Grace dealt with reality and not wishful thinking. Wishing did not give you six extra inches in height, or hair that wasn't baby-fine and didn't frizz in the rain.

Grace shook back her freshly blow-dried hair so that it fell river-straight and silky around her shoulders and down her narrow back. There was a hint of defiance in her face as she stared at her reflection in the full-length mirror.

She was not dressing for Theo, she told herself firmly.

'I'm dressing for myself, and this is not a date,' she announced to the room.

Which was probably just as well. She'd never been very good at dates—perhaps through her inability to read the room, or maybe just men. She had dressed up for George and had thought he was attracted to her, and look how well that had turned out.

She pushed away those thoughts and told herself that looking good was about confidence and feeling good about herself. She focused on her reflection, smoothing down the dress, and feeling quite pleased with what she saw.

She might not be a clothes horse, but she always felt good in this dress, because it made her look as if she actually had hips and elongated her legs.

It looked way better with heels, obviously, but that was not an option. So Grace embraced her vertical challenge in a slim pair of slingbacks, butter-soft, with a barely-there kitten heel, which were beautiful and kind to her ankle.

Giving her reflection one last critical look, she tried a swish of her blonde hair and stopped dead.

Why is your stomach cramped in knots, Grace? Why are you even joining Theo for supper?

Because he had asked.

Which in itself was strange—the asking part, at least. To her mind he was more of an ultimatum man, she decided. An image of his tall dark personage floated through her head, accompanied by an upping of the intensity in the uncomfortable shivery feeling in the pit of her belly.

The man had saved her life, so she reasoned it would have been churlish, under the circumstances, not to agree to eat with him. And today he had seemed less confrontational—less *dangerous*.

The word slipped into her head unbidden, and she shivered. If there was a way to break this standoff that didn't involve her giving in, obviously, she was not going to allow her antipathy to get in the way.

To be honest, if antipathy had been the only gut reaction she had towards Theo there wouldn't have been so much of a problem—but it wasn't.

There was no point in pretending that she was immune to his aura of sheer raw masculinity. The way he had of making a glance feel like a caress. And his sensuous mouth was...

She inhaled and closed down this dangerous line of thought. She intended to keep it closed this evening—it was just a casual dinner.

She glanced down, a frown pleating her brow. So maybe she was going overboard with the dress?

She dismissed the idea. It didn't matter what she was wearing—this was about listening. Ultra-wary of his apparent change of attitude, she was quite prepared not to like what she heard. And there was still a big question mark over his motivation. But there was only one way to find out.

She didn't want to be early and appear eager—which she really *wasn't*—so she took her time and an indirect route, which took her past Salvatore's study.

The door was ajar.

The eyes of the portrait on the wall seemed to follow her as she stepped into the room and over to the desk, where the papers she had started sorting at the start of the week were still stacked in piles. She ran a hand over the chair where Salvatore had sat and felt a deep welling of sadness that the man had gone but his paperwork remained.

When Marta had tentatively suggested that she begin to go through his papers Grace had been reluctant. It had felt like an intrusion. But she could see the logic of the request. If she didn't, who would?

Well, now maybe his son would. It was one of the things she would ask this evening.

She sat down—not in Salvatore's chair, but in a smaller, straight-backed version—with her back to the portrait and her elbows on the desk. She glanced at the clock on the wall opposite and one of her elbows slipped on the shiny polished surface of the desk, sending a stack of the assorted papers awaiting her attention sliding to the floor.

She swore softly and pushed her chair back. Then, anchoring the curtain of her hair away from her face with one forearm, she began to gather them up and return them to the desk.

The last item she retrieved was a slim leatherbound book. As she picked it up a scrap of paper that appeared to have been used as a bookmark fluttered out of it. After retrieving that too, she saw that it was not a piece of paper at all, but a snapshot, its glossy finish faded and dulled with years of handling.

Leaning back in her chair, Grace looked at it.

How old would Theo have been when it was taken? Eight or nine, maybe? He was dressed up in a shirt and tie, his youthful face shiny and scrubbed, and the woman whose hand he was holding was waving at the camera. Theo was not looking at the camera. He was looking up at the woman. His mother.

The expression on his youthful face made her throat thicken with emotion. She could not even begin to imagine the empty space that losing a mother at such an early age would leave in a child's life—the empty space where a mother should be.

It was so unfair, she reflected with a deep sigh. She might complain about her parents, but she knew how lucky she was to have them.

As she took hold of the book, to slide the photo back inside, it fell open at a page crowded with close-spaced writing in a hand she recognised as Salvatore's.

She paused, a sentence leaping out at her from the page.

Have I done the right thing?

She half closed the book. She already knew from the papers she had begun to sort out that Salvatore had used English in his private papers—the ones he presumably hadn't wanted any of the staff to catch a glimpse of.

She fingered the tooled leather and then opened it again, impelled by the tug of Pandora's box.

A word or two, she decided, maybe a sentence.

She ignored the guilty twinge as she bent over the open book.

Half an hour later she turned a page and saw that it was empty. Flicking through the pages, she saw that the rest of the book was too.

She turned back to the first page and saw the smudges where her tears had fallen. She glanced at the snapshot before sliding it back inside, her heart aching for every person involved in the real-life drama she had just been given a glimpse into.

Salvatore's love for his son had leapt from the page, as had his love for his wife, who came across as fragile and damaged. Clearly Salvatore had made a choice that had tortured him. Had he been right? Who was she to say, standing here years in the future? But it was hard not to think that had he not tried to protect his son from the truth things might be very different now... Theo might be very different.

'What are you doing?'

So engrossed in the tragedy of the past, Grace had lost all sense of place and time, and she jumped a mile. Looking, she knew, the picture of guilt, she turned to face the hostile figure looming in the doorway.

For a second his eyes were on the portrait on the wall, and she glimpsed a world of pain in them before it was gone, and then he was looking at her, his brow lightly furrowed, the suspicion in his eyes hardening.

She reacted to an instinctive impulse and tried to conceal the book clumsily behind her back.

'What is that?' he said, looking dark and dangerous and deeply suspicious as he stalked, lean and pantherlike, into the room.

There was something buried beneath the compassion she felt for him that reacted in an irrational or maybe simply a hormonal level to the aura of maleness he projected.

She stretched her stiff lips into a smile and got to her feet, disarranging the papers with a casual sweep of her hand and burying the book beneath the pile.

As he walked forward, casting her a stare of smouldering contempt, Grace's sinking heart told her that her sleight of hand was no good, and she was only delaying the inevitable.

And not for long.

His brown fingers went unerringly to the leatherbound diary, which he extracted.

His thumb flicked at the gold-edged pages. 'What is this?'

'A diary,' she said.

'A diary?' he echoed. His eyes went to her pale face and some of the tension left his own. 'Yours?'

He reached to hand it back to her—then dropped it when she shook her head.

'Your father's…' she whispered.

'And what sort of incriminating evidence does it hold, *cara*, that you are so anxious for me not to read it? What did Salvatore write about you?' he asked, feeling a surge of self-contempt.

He had almost relaxed his guard, due to his interest in what lay under that blue silk. It had caused him to forget that the owner of the big blue eyes and the supple seductive curves was the woman who had caused Salvatore—who worshipped at the altar of family and heritage—to split his estate.

That was quite a power, and it required a degree of cunning that it would be a mistake for him to overlook—*his* mistake, and one he was not about to repeat. Sex made some men blind, but not him.

Grace closed her eyes and sighed. 'It's not about me. It's an old diary, and I don't think you should read it, Theo,' she said, and she was almost pleading now as she watched him.

His upper lip curled. 'I had noticed that,' he drawled nastily.

She heaved a big sigh, as if recognising the inevitable, and as she looked at him with big compassionate eyes, bright with unshed tears, she nodded to the big French doors that opened onto the lawn.

'I'll wait outside for you. I'll be just there.'

He didn't respond beyond flinging her a frigid look of seething contempt. He had already taken his father's chair at the desk.

CHAPTER EIGHT

THE NIGHT WAS WARM, but Grace was shivering as she stared out at the distant gleam of the sea, her nerves too strung out to find the soft murmur of the wind in the pine trees soothing.

The ratcheting tension made her unable to keep still. She moved with restless energy across the grass, back and forth, starting at the slightest sound, turning intermittently to look at the illuminated fairy tale facade of the palazzo with the starlit sky backdrop that gave it its name.

She almost leapt out of her skin when she heard a loud crashing sound from inside the room. She took an impulsive step and then hesitated, before deciding to stay where she was. He would probably tell her to go away—probably not in polite terms, she reflected with a rueful half-smile.

But he was making a life-changing discovery, and no one should be alone at such a moment—even a man like Theo, who came across as someone so self-contained. Which, considering the number of women's names that had come up when she had typed his name into a search engine, might seem an odd description, but it was one that fitted.

Well, now she knew the closely guarded secret—she knew what had caused the rift between father and son, and it was a tragic story.

She now knew, from reading the diary entries, that she was not the only person at the palazzo who was aware of the full story. But they had been sworn to silence by Salvatore. It was a measure of their loyalty and respect for the man that no one had breathed a word after his death.

They had protected Salvatore's secret.

His pain had leapt off the page as he'd described the moment when he'd decided to conceal the truth. They were words that Grace knew she would never forget.

Theo is hurting. I could see the hate in his eyes. I opened my mouth to defend myself, to tell him I would never cheat on his mother, and then I realised what that would mean.

Better he hates me than his mother. I couldn't protect her in life, but I can protect

*her in death. A child can never understand
that a parent is human, has weaknesses.*

*If only I had realised what was in her
mind...*

*I cannot risk the suicide note being dis-
covered. I will burn it.*

*I have asked Marta never to mention it.
I know she won't.*

It broke Grace's heart to think of father and
son both hurting.

Salvatore's instinct to protect his wife's memory and the love his young son had meant that
he had lied when the young Theo—trauma-
tised after his mother had taken her life—had
put his own interpretation on the snatches of a
conversation he'd overheard.

*'She just couldn't live with the shame of the
affair.'*

It had never crossed his mind that his mother
was living with the shame of her *own* affair.

The diary entry had explained that being unable even to go to the funeral of her married
lover had sent the emotionally fragile woman
into a deep spiral of depression that she had
never pulled out of.

Salvatore could have told the truth when con-
fronted by his young son. Instead he had taken
on the burden of guilt as his own.

She couldn't begin to imagine what Theo would be feeling as he read his father's thoughts, found the tenets he had built his adult life upon being deconstructed. It had to leave a person who dealt in certainties—indeed *any* person—feel adrift.

She walked some more, back and forth, wearing a groove in the neatly trimmed grass, and then the French doors opened. His hands on the double doors, he stood for a moment in the white light, curtains blowing behind him, a tall, broad-shouldered silhouette.

Then he saw her…paused before surging forward. It seemed at first as if he'd walk straight past her, but then at the last moment he stopped and turned to face her.

His face, normally lit by a vibrant glow, was tinged with grey, strain written into every line. At a moment like this she knew that he needed someone not involved…someone objective… Sadly Grace didn't feel objective at all. Her heart was aching for him.

'Did you know?' he asked abruptly, his voice a low growl as he stepped back.

Grace saw that since she had left the room he had discarded his jacket. His dark, normally sleek hair stood in spiky disarray around his face, as though he had run his fingers through it multiple times, and several of the buttons on his shirt had come adrift, enough to reveal a section of his muscled chest.

'No, not until just now, when I read what your father had written. But, Theo…' His head turned from his brooding contemplation of the starlit sky. 'I did know how much your father loved you.'

He suddenly raised clenched hands to his temples, and his laugh sounded like glass breaking. 'Well, that makes it all right, then. Sorry…' he ground out, clenching his jaw.

'It's fine,' she said, in her best objective observer voice, seeing through his anger to the pain beneath.

'I can't believe this. All these years… Why the hell would he do that?' He swung back to her once more. 'He stood in that room when I was kid and I told him I hated him. I called him— The things I said— And he just stood there and took it. *Why?*'

He groaned, and the sound was almost one of animalistic pain that made her want to cover her ears.

'Why didn't he just say that it was *her* affair…*her* shame? She had to have been cheating on him for years. He *lived* with her. He *knew* about her infidelity. And yet he— Why did he let me think that he—?'

He was shaking his head, and she could see

him digging deep for control, gathering his considerable resources before he turned back.

'This has nothing to do with you. I'm sorry. It's not your problem. It's just that you were... here...'

'Salvatore made it my problem when for his own reasons—which we might never know— he named me in his will,' Grace reminded him quietly. 'So, you see, I am now involved.'

'You had no part in the lie I have been living most of my life...hating the man. He was right you know,' he added.

'Right...?'

A muscle clenched in his jaw. 'I would have hated her.'

He flung the words at her almost like a challenge.

'You were a child, Theo.' Her heart ached for his pain. 'And your mother was not well.'

'Is that what you call cheating on your husband?'

'She was in love.'

'Are you defending her?'

'Parents are just people...like you and me. They're not perfect. I'm sure your mother loved your father too, in a different way, and she *did* love you,' she added sadly, thinking of the tragic figure in the portrait. 'I suppose you can't pick who you love.'

He was staring at her with an intensity that was hard to bear but she didn't look away. Her heart twisted painfully in her chest when she tried to imagine what he must be feeling at this moment.

'She didn't love him *or* me.'

The words seemed wrenched from him against his will.

'Oh, no!' she exclaimed stepping forward.

She hesitated a moment before reaching up to place her hand palm flat against the rigid muscles of his upper arm, letting it lie there.

She doubted he even registered it.

'I've seen the photos. She *adored* you. And your father... Well, maybe they drifted apart, or she couldn't love him in the way he loved her. It happens.'

Something in her voice seemed to penetrate his black mood and made him look at her sharply. 'It's happened to you?'

She thought about lying, or not saying anything more, but decided that if focusing on her messed-up life took his mind off his own she could live with having her privacy invaded.

She nodded. 'I thought he loved me, but he didn't...' She swallowed. 'Except as a sister,' she added.

'And now?'

'We're friends now. He married my sister.'

'And you are all right with that?' he asked incredulously.

'I don't have a lot of choice.'

'What a bastard!'

She gave a light laugh. 'Now, that *would* make it easier,' she admitted wryly, beginning to feel embarrassed that she had shared something so private. 'But actually George is awfully nice. And she's my sister. It's not like I could—' She stopped, a self-conscious expression drifting across her face.

'Not like you could cut her out of your life? You'd be surprised how easy it is,' he drawled. 'I'm the expert.'

'I didn't mean that.'

Theo inhaled, his chest lifting as he stared blankly straight ahead, and then he said abruptly, 'Salvatore...' He paused. 'My father...'

It was as if not even in the privacy of his own thoughts had he used the word for a very long time.

'He's dead, and I will never— We will never be able to— I was a child, but now— He took that choice away from me.'

'I know,' she said, every cell in her body

aching at the suffering etched in his face. 'But your father loved you.'

Her soft, calm voice seemed to be getting through the maelstrom of emotions that must be gripping him.

'And he knew that deep down you loved him. I'm sure of it. I can't judge his choice. I think he judged himself. But he thought he was doing the right thing. He struggled with it, but in the end he didn't want to tarnish the love you had for her mother. He wanted to protect your memories of her.'

She felt some of the tension in his bulging biceps relax a notch.

'I understand that you're angry.'

'Understand?'

She winced at the snarled response.

'No, you're right,' she admitted. 'I have no idea how you're feeling—how could I?'

His expression softened fractionally as he looked down at her face. 'I don't know how I'm feeling,' he admitted with a wry twist of his lips as he lifted his gaze, looking out into the distance towards the sea. 'He went to his grave letting me think that he killed my mother—that the shame that drove her to take her life was the fact that *he* was unfaithful.'

Grace didn't respond. She didn't think he expected her to.

'It's such a bloody unholy mess…' He jabbed his long fingers into his dark pelt of hair, leaving a few extra sexy spikes when he lowered them. 'The times I have thought of this place…'

'You love it, don't you?' she said, not realising she had voiced her discovery out loud until he tipped his head sharply to stare down at her.

'I have a Welsh friend… They have a word for it: *hiraeth*—there's no translation in English,' he added, turning his gaze to the dark outline of the distant mountains against the night sky. 'But it means a tug…a *yearning* for a place or a feeling that is lost. Something that can never be revisited—a kind of deep longing… homesickness tinged with sorrow.'

She felt tears prick her eyes. She suspected this was the first time he had admitted, even to himself, his emotional connection to this place.

'And now you're home,' she said softly.

His home—not hers, she reminded herself as he glanced down at her, looking startled by her comment, as though the idea had not occurred to him. But it would. If not now, then soon, she was sure.

He might not realise it yet, but there was no reason for Theo to reject his birthright any longer—which meant there was no reason for her to be here.

And when she had left—when this was all

a memory and she was back nursing, which she loved—would she feel a sense of what he was describing? This...*hiraeth*? Could a person grow that close to somewhere in such a short space of time?

People fell in love in a short space of time, or so she had heard.

She had known George for a year before she'd decided her warm feelings for him were love.

These days she wondered if that 'love' hadn't just been having someone who listened to what she was saying and looked interested. As a person who came from a family where everyone was more knowledgeable than she was, Grace was used to having her opinion drowned out in any conversation. It had been quite intoxicating to have someone hear what she was saying.

But when she'd looked at George she had never felt the sort of sexual hunger that she did when she looked at Theo.

'We haven't eaten,' he said.

She blinked and shook her head, admitting, 'I'd forgotten.'

Getting dressed that evening, knowing there was only one person she was trying to impress, feeling that little illicit thrill of excitement in the pit of her belly that she wouldn't acknowledge but enjoyed, seemed a lifetime ago.

'I'm not really hungry now.'

He didn't force it, and she reasoned he probably wanted to be alone. He had a lot to process.

'I— Well— Goodnight,' she said suddenly unable to meet his eyes.

It hadn't been easy, but she had been able to fight her powerful attraction to his dark, brooding looks. Glimpsing his vulnerability had cut through all her defences.

'I'm glad he had you for those last weeks.'

Theo looked as surprised to hear himself delivering the comment as Grace felt receiving it.

'He was not in pain,' she said, hoping that made him feel better.

'Good. But I meant that you… I think your company must have made his last days… I'm glad he was not alone.'

His eyes were drawn to her mouth, and he felt a quiver of lust as his glance lingered on the lush, quivering outline.

'I enjoyed his company—*just* his company,' she said, flushing. An antagonistic glitter appeared in her electric blue eyes as she lifted her chin. 'No matter what the tabloids say. I suppose you've read the article?'

'I don't read tabloids,' he said, not adding that he didn't have to.

There were people in his employ who did it

for him—people, in this instance, who planted the stories to begin with.

'Shame not everyone follows your example,' she said.

'Their numbers are falling all the time, and nobody believes what they read,' he said, finding himself unable to meet her eyes.

She smiled, appreciating his attempt to make her feel better.

'I wish that were true—' she began, then promptly lost her thread as their glances collided and held.

It was as if some invisible force had her in its grip.

Grace had never felt anything like it.

The air quivered as the elusive attraction between them flared and grew hot.

If only life was as simple and uncomplicated as lust, Theo mused, feeling its tug. For once he didn't push back against it. He let it envelop him, heat his blood, awaken his senses and fill his head.

Looking at her mouth, he didn't have to think…he didn't have to sift through the maze of emotions that today's discovery had shaken free.

In the space of time it had taken for him to

read those handwritten pages everything Theo had believed had slipped away. He felt as though he was walking through quicksand. For years when he'd thought of his father it had been with a flat, cold anger—anger that was still there. He felt cheated…mortified… And the first scratches of guilt were like nails on a blackboard.

His jaw clenched as he tried to block the emotional gut-punch.

Staring at her mouth was, he discovered, a way of silencing the angry buzz of thoughts swirling in his head.

Grace was no longer trying to break eye contact with Theo. He was still staring at her. With an expression in his dark eyes that made her heart rate quicken and her knees shake a little.

'It must be a lot to take in,' she said, feeling impelled to say something, even if it did sound trite.

She had to cut through this new tension that buzzed in the air between them.

'Tomorrow,' he said. 'I don't want to take it in tonight.'

Tonight he wanted to bury himself in her soft body and experience the uncomplicated, mind-numbing pleasure of sex.

* * *

Grace wanted to look away, but she couldn't. Her throat was dry, her heart was hammering, and the fist of desire in her chest was making it hard for her to breathe as she looked up at him with eyes that were feverishly jewel-bright.

'What do you want to do tonight?'

Hearing the words that fell from her lips… hearing a voice she barely recognised as her own…she suddenly experienced a moment's panic.

What if she was reading this wrong?

'The same thing as you.'

She gave him a long, level look. 'You don't know what I want.'

'I like a challenge.'

He smiled, then. It was not a gentle smile—it was dark and dangerous and it made her shake.

'I'm open to instruction.'

His fingers were gentle as they cupped her chin, drawing her face up to his, one hand stroking her hair as he bent down and fitted his mouth to hers.

There was a desperation and a terrifying need in his kiss that lit something inside her. With a half-moan, half-sob, Grace fell into him, grabbing at his shirt, hooking her fingers into the nape of his neck, to drag herself close. She pressed her body against his hard, muscular chest, revelling in the exciting solidity of his lean body.

He answered her aggression by increasing the pressure of his thrusting tongue, opening her mouth wider, until she felt as though he would consume her.

Then he found her breast, his hand curving across the small mound, moulding it, while softening the kiss until it was a slow, aching, gentle torment.

By this point Grace's brain had stopped functioning. Instinct and blind hunger were in charge. She was just along for the ride. Her knees had buckled and she was floating...holding on for dear life.

He drew his head back for a moment and looked down at her face, his glazed eyes half closed, his face flushed, his delicious lips parted against her mouth.

'You are perfect,' he breathed, tracing a slow and not quite steady path with one finger down her jaw. 'I need you. I need *this*...' he groaned.

'I need this too,' she said, breathing as hard as he was.

His dark eyes flared with a primitive satisfaction as he picked her up.

She didn't protest. She just linked her arms around his neck as he strode towards the illuminated building.

CHAPTER NINE

'YOUR PLACE OR MINE?' he said as he turned and, still carrying her, shouldered his way through a side door and then a small corridor that was dimly lit by a row of shaded wall lights.

'Whichever is nearer.'

'Good thinking,' he said, with a fierce smile that melted her bones. 'Then yours it is. I want to kiss you some more, but if I do we won't get to your bedroom. And I don't think our first time should be on a back staircase. But please know,' he added, taking the stairs in question two at a time, 'that I am thinking about kissing you. I am thinking about kissing every inch of you.'

When they got there her room was just the way she'd left it. But she was very different.

She was about to take a lover!

And not before time, said the voice in her head.

Theo walked over to the four-poster bed and

haphazardly pulled back the pretty quilt, before laying her on her back across the bed and kneeling above her, his hands either side of her face.

'Now...' he said, trailing a series of butterfly kisses along her jaw. 'Those kisses I owe you, *cara*...'

Neck extended, back arched, her head pushed deep into the mattress, she lay there with her eyes closed. And above her head her fingers curled while he kissed his way down the swan-like column of her throat, along her jaw. He paused as he reached her mouth, staring down at her before he claimed it, tasting and teasing, tugging sensuously, as if filling his mouth with the taste of her and letting her taste him.

Grace felt the flames inside her getting hotter as the kiss deepened. She lowered her arms in order to slide them around his ribcage, locking them against his spine as she kissed him back, meeting his exploring tongue and opening her mouth wide to deepen the penetration.

She strained upwards, pressing her aching breasts against his chest as they rolled over, locked together, his hands in her hair, then on her body. She was on fire.

She gave a murmur of protest as his mouth pulled away.

His eyes were smoky and hot. 'Just let me...'

She watched as he fought his way out of his shirt, finally flinging it aside. She sucked in a breath through her flared nostrils and arched up to lay her hands flat against his hard, ridged belly, feeling the illusion of control as the muscles there contracted.

She knew it was an illusion because she had never felt less in control in her life.

It was an incredible feeling.

'You are totally beautiful,' she told him throatily. 'I bet you get told that a lot… You *feel* beautiful.'

One hand braced on the mattress, she raised herself upwards to press her mouth to his belly, allowing her tongue to move across his skin.

'You taste…' She tilted her head back to direct a sultry look up at him through her lashes. 'Salty.'

Her head dipped forward once more, but his hands tangling in her hair pulled her away. Ignoring her growl of discontent, he pushed her back to the mattress.

She fell and lay there, breathing hard. Sitting astride her, he looked down into her hectically flushed face.

'My turn, I think,' he said, laying one hand flat on the blue silk that covered her belly. 'Nice dress…but you look hot.'

She nodded fervently, then let out a low moan

when he covered one breast with his hand, rubbing the engorged nipple with his thumb.

He peeled the straps down her shoulders and gave a low, feral groan. There was a husky reverence in his tone as he pulled her body up against his, hunger in his face, and rasped, 'Just perfect.'

Her quivering insides liquefied as she wound her arms around his neck, and she was so involved in being excited by the skin-to-skin contact that she had no idea how she ended up lying on her side, face to face with him…thigh to thigh.

Her body moved urgently against his as his hands slid down between them to touch her through the silk, while the clever pull of his lips against her mouth, the stroke of his tongue, made her moan and whimper, then guide his hand back to a place that she liked.

Theo felt his control, his sanity, slipping from his grip. She was more responsive to his touch than any woman he had ever been with. Her sensuality was innate, and her sensitivity to his lightest touch sent hunger roaring through him like an out-of-control forest fire, burning him up.

He was aware of a growing possessiveness in him as he looked at her. Something that he had never felt with a woman before. It was an almost primeval need to claim her as his own, and he knew the feeling was linked not just to the beautiful body that drove him insane but the whole person she was.

'My beautiful…' his hand slid to her deliciously rounded little bottom, kneading the firm flesh '…wanton…' he watched the rapid rise and fall of her small, perfect, quivering breasts as he located the zip of her dress and tugged it smoothly down '…angel,' he rasped, punctuating each word with a deep, downing kiss.

Her eyes fluttered open as he pulled the dress down in one smooth motion.

'Just cooling you down.'

Except of course he wasn't.

Grace was not cool at all.

She was burning up with a need that was like nothing she had ever imagined.

In addition to the dark prickles under the surface of her ultra-sensitised skin, she felt her core temperature shifting several degrees higher.

She watched him, her head propped on her elbow, her breathing shallow and uneven, as he held her eyes and freed himself of his tailored trousers, only dropping her gaze when the zipper got stuck as he dragged it over his erection.

The bulging outline in his boxers suggested

why there had been some issues. Her cheeks were stinging pink as he dragged her towards him, his expression tense. She didn't want to say anything or do anything to break the spell. She just stared back. Words had little meaning anyway. She didn't have the vocabulary to describe what she was feeling and the total, absolute and earth-shattering *rightness* of it.

He stroked her hair, the tenderness in his touch in stark contrast to the ferocity drawn in his hard-boned dark face. She felt the tension of being in the eye of a storm, the false calm before all hell broke loose—or in this case all *heaven*.

Then, as his glance drifted to her mouth, he began to kiss her again, stroking into the warm recesses of her mouth, dragging her into him, sealing their bodies at the hip while he kissed her, trailing kisses down her throat until he reached her breast.

Ignoring, actually enjoying, the abrasive rasp of his stubble against her skin, she slid her fingers into his hair and held him there. She tried to press in harder and, sensing her frustration, he stopped, pulling her thigh across his so that, without thinking, she rubbed the aching damp core of her sex against him, feeling the desperation build inside her as they lay there in a tangle of sweet, slick limbs and gasps and moans.

She was so involved in what she was feeling that she barely registered her silk panties were gone until he slid a finger into her wet heat.

'You are so tight,' he murmured against her mouth.

'Am I?' she whispered dragging her foot down the back of his leg as she breathed in the warm, earthy smell of his arousal.

'It's been a long time for you?'

The idea that she had not got over this George person filled him with a fierce, savage determination that he would make her forget the man ever existed.

'Sort of…'

She nodded, closing her eyes as he curved his hand over one breast, making a sound of throaty appreciation when he discovered it fitted perfectly in his hand.

His appreciation had apparently given her confidence, because she admitted in a rush, 'Actually, not a long time…more never.'

It took a few seconds for her meaning to penetrate, at which point he froze and lifted his head to look at her, the dark ridges along his cheekbones emphasising the sybaritic cast of his sculpted features.

'You're saying…?'

* * *

Grace nodded, thinking that if he rejected her now—

She found herself unable even to think that far ahead—but she could almost taste the desolation she would feel. It would be nothing remotely like the way she had felt when George had rejected her—that would be like comparing a flickering candle flame to a full-blown forest fire...

'Oh, *cara*...' he crooned throatily, stroking her face with a tenderness that was in stark contrast to the smoky passion in his eyes. 'Are you sure you want this now...with me...?'

The answer came easily to her.

She wanted him—all of him, only him—here and now.

'Very sure.'

'I will make it good for you, I promise.'

She watched through her lashes as he divested himself of his boxers, drinking in the sight of his body, which was an essay in male perfection—not an ounce of surplus flesh to disguise the muscular ripples that defined every muscle and sinew of his long greyhound-lean body.

When he rolled towards her again, bringing

himself closer, he traced the dip of her waist and the gentle female flare of her hip with a finger.

He stared at her, wanting to lose himself in her, the need so strong that he hesitated.

She was so small, so fragile…

He kissed her collar bone, her mouth…

He was afraid that he would break her.

But her passion was bigger than her frame, and the knowledge darkened his eyes with passion.

She made him think of a sleek and supple little cat…

Her breath quickened in anticipation as she saw his eyes darken.

'I need you,' he said.

'Please, yes…'

Her breath left her body in a long, soundless gasp as he slid into her. Her eyes squeezed closed, blanking out everything, including the expressive series of shadows that moved across his clenched features.

Everything but the exquisite sensation of him filling her slowly, slowly, until she had all of him.

She could fill the tension inside her build as he moved, his strokes faster and deeper. She could not match his technique, nor his powers of seduction, so she just held on for the ride. And then she arrived with an explosion of sensation so intense she didn't know where she began and he ended…it was just one pulsing explosion of pleasure that made them one.

Her sex-soaked brain came lazily back to life as she drifted down to earth, her body racked by pleasurable little aftershocks.

She kept her eyes closed. She knew she had to be careful not to project her feelings onto Theo. But it wasn't easy. She wanted to scream…yell it from the rooftops. Everything felt so good and so special, so utterly perfect, that she wanted to share—though in this case she knew it would be an overshare.

'Are you asleep, Grace?'

'Yes.'

She almost was—and anyhow, she definitely wasn't awake enough for a post-coital post-mortem over why he was her first lover.

If she hadn't told him, would he have noticed? He might not have. She thought for a beginner she had not been bad, and hopefully what she'd lacked in technique she had made up for in enthusiasm.

'B plus,' she mumbled.

'What was that?'

'I didn't say anything.'

* * *

Theo laughed and stared down at her face, stroking her soft cheek for a while before sliding down the bed, pressing her face into his shoulder and adjusting his body as she curled into him.

This was not an intimacy he had ever allowed himself—it was not a tenderness that he had wanted—but it felt *right*.

He was too tired to analyse its rightness…

When Grace woke it was still dark, and Theo was wide awake, looking down at her.

'You're leaving?' she asked.

'Do you want me to?'

She shook her head.

'Good.'

He kissed her—a long, dreamy kiss that she felt all the way down to her curling toes. Then, to her annoyance he pulled away, propping himself on one elbow.

'So—before you distract me—what,' he asked, 'was wrong with your George?'

She didn't misunderstand his meaning. 'Maybe I should have mentioned before—?'

He rolled his eyes. 'That you were a virgin? *Maybe?* Seriously, Grace?'

The shock still hadn't worn off. Nor had the knowledge that he had found it arousing to be her first lover—arousing and incomprehensible, considering her innate sensuality.

'Last night you needed sex,' Grace said.

And she had been handy, she knew.

'And I needed to— Well, I needed— You get to a certain age and it's— People think there's something wrong with you if you've not had a lover. And there's the whole "do you mention it on the first date or—?" Look,' she said touching her hot cheeks. 'I'm blushing and I've seen you naked.'

He still was, she assumed, her glance sliding to the sheet that was gathered around his narrow waist.

'Last night with you…it didn't feel awkward.'

Something flashed in his eyes, but Grace almost missed the moment as her eyes closed in concentration while she tried to find the right words.

'I didn't overthink, and it just felt…well, really perfect.'

'I can see that you overthink things sometimes.'

Anxious that this was his way of telling her not to read anything deep and meaningful into last night, she agreed quickly. 'Absolutely.'

'And before George?'

'Men say I'm too nice. They think of me as a sister. And I'm not very highly sexed.'

His lips quirked as they slid to her breasts above the covers. 'Believe me, Grace, they do *not* think of you like a sister and we both know there is nothing wrong with your sex drive. I think your problem is more common than you might think. Men are daunted by beautiful, smart women. You intimidate them.'

Grace stared at him, waiting for the punchline—it didn't come.

Theo Ranieri, the most gorgeous man on the planet, thought she was beautiful, smart and also sexy?

She lowered her lashes, hugging this extraordinary knowledge to herself.

'This George of yours…' He shook his head.

'George respected me,' she said primly.

'George sounds like a loser. Does he have sex with your sister? Or is theirs a pure and elevated love? A meeting of minds such that they only read poetry to one another?'

'They have a child,' she retorted.

'Immaculate conception?'

She swatted at him and found it amazing that she was naked, laughing with Theo Ranieri, and it felt normal.

'George does write poetry though.' She couldn't keep her laughter in. 'Very bad poetry. But seriously, I don't think George ever actually fancied me.'

'The man is a loser.'

'Will you stop saying that? We were waiting...'

'For what? He sounds like a loser to me.'

'He slept with my sister the first night they met.'

She spoke matter-of-factly, even managed a soft laugh, but at the time the discovery had been devastating and had sent her confidence to an all-time low.

'He had come home with me to meet my parents. He gave her a lift home and they made out in the back seat.'

'Oh, very classy!' Theo sneered, adding, 'He *told* you this?'

'She told me. George just didn't fancy me.'

Now she knew that the feeling had been mutual—what she had felt for George had been friendship, though she hadn't known it at the time. Back then, she hadn't known what passion was...what the need to lose yourself in someone could feel like...that surrender could feel so powerful.

That you could feel a never-ending fascination for a man's body.

And the discovery was still all new and wonderful.

She ran her hand down his flank, letting it

rest possessively on his behind, loving the fact that he was all sinew and muscle.

He blew out a heavy breath. 'It sounds like a match made in heaven.'

'My sister is very beautiful, successful—and scarily smart.'

'I'm sure she would agree with that assessment. I met her once.'

Grace tensed. 'Did you sleep with her?'

The question was out of her mouth before her self-censoring facility had kicked in.

'Sleep with her?' He laughed. 'I can't honestly remember what the woman looked like,' he admitted. 'But what struck me most was her pig-headed confidence that she was right about—I think—everything. It must be nice to be so utterly convinced of your own infallibility.'

She was struck with how right he was about Hope, who never suffered a moment's doubt. Though, considering its source, the comment struck Grace as uniquely funny.

'You should know!'

She stopped, a look of horror spreading across her face, as she realised how after this evening's events that was the wrong joke to make on so many levels.

'Relax,' he soothed.

'If I hadn't found that diary and read it you wouldn't know.'

And we might not be in bed.

Actually, strike the *might*. He had reached out last night because he'd wanted to forget, and she had been handy.

Ready and willing, mocked the voice in her head.

'I'm glad you did. I'm glad I know.'

Grace wasn't sure she believed him—she had witnessed his devastation last night.

He read the doubt in her face. 'Everyone deserves the truth, no matter how painful that truth is. Without the truth you can't make an informed decision. I have based all my decisions on a lie. Oh, I know why he—my father—lied, but it was wrong.'

She reached out and touched his shoulder.

'For a billionaire workaholic, you sound very grounded,' she added naughtily.

His eyes crinkling at the corners, he threw back his head and laughed.

She watched with approval. 'Maybe laughter isn't *the* best medicine,' she said. 'But it's up there…just underneath wild, head-banging sex.'

She felt his eyes on her face. He wasn't smiling or laughing. He was looking tense—she could almost see the tension radiating out of his warm body.

'Did I say that out loud?'

'I happen to be in complete agreement with you on the subject,' he purred, rolling over on one elbow as he pushed her fair hair back from her face. 'They say abstinence is character-building, but I'm willing to take the risk if you are.'

He leaned forward, but Grace held her hand against his, preventing him from kissing her, knowing that once he did she'd be toast and she'd never ask.

'I hope you don't mind me asking, Theo,' she began hesitantly, 'but last night…things are a bit…well, blurry. And I was a bit focused on—Well, the thing is, did you take precautions?'

The expressions flickering across his face settled into tenderness. 'I did use a condom. I would never be so selfish as to risk an unwanted pregnancy. You can relax. I will look after you. Will you trust me to do that, *cara*?'

'Of course!' It was not something she even needed to think about.

For some reason she couldn't fathom, her response made him scowl and look severe. 'You are safe with me, but you shouldn't be so trusting—not all men are so careful with their partners.'

She started to sit up. 'Can I wait until you kick me out of the bed before I go looking for your replacement?' she enquired acidly. 'Do you want to vet him or run a security check?'

'Calm down,' he said, placing a restraining hand on her breast. 'No insult intended. I know you can look after yourself. I've been on the receiving end of your incinerate-at-fifty-paces stare.'

He veiled his eyes so that the lingering effects of a stab of jealousy so intense it had felt like a blade sliding between his ribs might not show in his face.

A stab of jealousy that had spurred him into unhelpful speech.

That, and the image of some faceless future lover enjoying the passion *he* had unlocked made him feel physically sick.

The militant light faded from Grace's eyes as she realised the lie in his words.

If I could look after myself I wouldn't have allowed myself to have feelings for my enemy... to sleep with him and to want to do it again.

She had never been in this situation before, but she was pretty sure that at some point there was going to be pain and regret involved.

The really scary part was that she didn't care.

The bittersweet knowledge added another layer to her emotions as they made love again, and this time it was less frantic. It was still passionate, but tender, and Theo was considerate of her body, which ached in places she hadn't known could ache.

This time he fulfilled his unrealistic intention of kissing every inch of her body and then some, and coached her in how to touch him, to drive him to edge and then back again, building her confidence and increasing her fascination with his hard, lean body.

He seemed reluctant to leave the heat of her body after they had both climaxed, and Grace had no issue with the way his heavy body felt against hers. Sliding in and out of an exhausted sleep, she had no idea how long they stayed that way.

When Grace woke up fully, she was alone and it was daytime.

Talk about the cold light of day, she thought, feeling the mattress that bore the imprint and scent of him, but no Theo.

It was cold.

He was long gone.

CHAPTER TEN

SHE HAD WASHED, dressed, and donned a steely resolve not to be clingy along with double denim—which was probably a mistake. If last night had been a one-off, she told herself, embracing a 'laughing in the face of disaster' mentality was totally fine.

It was twelve thirty-one when Theo entered her room. She knew because she had been glancing at the time roughly every minute.

'Hello,' she said her smile extra-bright.

'I was just talking to Marta.'

'Oh?' Grace murmured vaguely, adopting an expression she hoped made it clear that she didn't think she was owed any explanation of his whereabouts, and she definitely *wasn't* keeping tabs on him.

She continued to line up her nail varnishes on the dressing table.

'I told her about the diary and asked her to fill in any blanks she was able to.'

'Oh!'

Grace abandoned her neat, geometrically precise line, and walked quickly over to him. 'How did it go?'

'She was upset, and things got pretty emotional. She was put in an impossible position by my father, and she imagined I would be angry—'

'But you weren't?' she cut in quickly.

'Hell, of course not! It seems that there were only six people who knew about the suicide note—it seems the affair was only ever believed to be a rumour. They were very discreet, apparently, and everyone knew that my mother had a history of mental health issues. This was a long time ago, and such things were spoken of in hushed whispers. Three of those staff who were in the know are dead, one has retired and gone to live with his son in Rome, my father's old butler has had a stroke and is in a care home, and that leaves Marta.'

'Is that good?'

'Not for the dead people or the old butler.'

She threw him a look. 'So that's it, then?'

'Marta is as much in the dark about the will as we are, but she has a theory. She thinks that he left you half the estate to bring me back here. Apparently he never stopped believing I belonged here. She tells me that he always believed that if I returned—even once—I would never leave.'

Grace swallowed past the emotional lump in her throat. 'And he was right, wasn't he?' she said quietly. 'You do belong here.'

'Maybe…' he said cautiously. 'I have a very different life now.'

'I don't believe you were ever going to sell. I think there would have come a point—'

'You're a romantic!' he accused.

'No!' she protested.

He flopped down with careless long-limbed elegance on a straight-backed chintzy sofa, winced, and surged back to his feet. 'That thing is like sitting on a concrete doorstep,' he complained.

'Well, you can get rid of it—make the place over to your liking. I'll sign whatever you want. Obviously, your father never really wanted the estate to go out of the family or be split. And I don't want to profit from it.'

Theo shook his head and wondered how he had ever thought this woman was a hustler. With her warm heart and generosity she was much more likely to be taken advantage of…to be a victim of some unscrupulous bastard.

'You're never going to be rich,' he told her.

She shrugged. 'I don't particularly want to be.'

'You love it here, don't you?'

'It's not my home,' she said, dodging his eyes.

'But it could be. Look, for the moment, why don't we just leave things as they are? It's never a good idea to make hasty decisions,' he said— the man who had once been quoted as saying that instinct won, hesitation lost. 'I have a life away from here. And the day-to-day running of the palazzo—'

'Nic,' she interrupted, 'is very capable.'

'Nic is expecting—well, his wife is expecting a new baby. He's already asked for a temporary reduction in hours.'

Theo still found it hard to think of his rebellious old friend as a hands-on dad.

'And according to him there is no one on his team who is at the stage of stepping up. He was telling me how relieved he is that you're around to take up the slack. As he pointed out, you don't mind hard work.'

She hesitated.

'So you're thinking I could be some sort of manager?' she said, and paused, flicking her low ponytail around her finger and letting it uncoil.

'You're not a manager—you are the co-owner.'

'Salvatore never really intended that,' she fretted.

'You can't know that. Look, let's call this a holding position until we both settle into the arrangement…play it by ear?'

And play by night, he thought, looking at her through the screen of his jet lashes.

'Think of it as a co-operative—that would suit your egalitarian principles.'

In the act of nudging a nail varnish bottle into line she spun around. 'How do you know I have egalitarian principles?'

'You're trying to give away a fortune. That is kind of a clue, *cara.*'

She needed protecting from herself, he decided, his eyes flickering to the bed, neatly made up with clean linen.

She slung him a cranky look and then pushed all the nail varnish bottles into a wastepaper bin with a sweep of her hand.

'I'm confused,' she snapped, and he half wondered if that wasn't the idea.

'All right, then. Let's get down to basics: stay until you get bored with screwing me.'

'Or you get bored with screwing me,' she returned, struggling to match his flippancy, and refusing to be fazed by the crudity.

The reality was she was shamefully aroused. She shifted her weight casually from one foot to the other, but it did nothing to relieve the ache between her legs.

A voice in her head was telling her that the time was fast approaching when she would not be able to disguise her emerging feelings. She took a deep breath. She just had to stay in control and enjoy every moment, savour them to think back on when she left.

'I think we have some time to go before that happens,' he said drily. 'Sex with you is the best sex I have ever experienced. I love it that you can blush after what we did last night. You have nothing to compare last night with, but let me tell you I have. And we're great in bed together. Or,' he added, with a wicked devil-on-steroids grin, 'just about anywhere. We could actually do it in all the rooms in the building. Have you been in the attics? It's a rabbit warren. But I draw a line at the cellars—they're creepy,' he admitted, his eyes dancing.

'Theo!' she gasped, thinking of all the rooms in the palazzo and getting hot and bothered.

'Grace…' he mocked. 'You're going to say yes—we both know it. You want me now, don't you?' he purred. 'You like it when I talk dirty…'

She said yes.

Luca Ferrara was one of Theo's oldest friends and also a bestselling author. Theo, it seemed, had introduced him to his wife, the American actress Sophia Halton.

The photogenic pair were so famous that they were known by a joint name: *Luphia*.

Tonight was to be a small 'intimate' gathering of a hundred or so of their 'closest' friends—their inner circle—to celebrate the actress's birthday. Sophia, who really did have everything, had requested donations to her favourite worthy cause rather than gifts.

The security was to be very tight. But although there would be no press or cameras allowed inside, the couple were allowing selected press to take photos of their guests arriving and leaving.

Mobile phones would be left at the door.

A big announcement was rumoured, and speculation had reached fever pitch that it would be the news of an imminent birth. It was no secret that the couple had been trying for a baby for years, and had been through several rounds of IVF with no good news at the end. So maybe Sophia didn't have it all?

Grace was one of the few people who knew the truth.

The announcement *was* about a baby—or rather two—and they were eighteen months old, twins, one born with a learning disability. The adoption had gone through the previous month, and the couple wanted to announce how happy they were with their new family.

All the pleasure Grace had felt when Theo had shared the secret with her had vanished when he had returned later that day specifically to remind her that the information was confidential, and his friends were relying on discretion from the few in the know.

As if he thought she was about to blab on social media!

She had swallowed the hurt, held her tongue, and despised herself for the careful restraint she displayed as she told him she understood. Which was true. She understood that Theo didn't really trust her, and this wasn't the first time the issue had shown itself in other ways over the past month.

Not big things, but they had a cumulative effect.

There'd been occasions when he had closed his laptop to prevent her seeing the screen when she walked into room, and she'd pretended not to notice. He could vanish for twenty-four hours without any explanation, and it never seemed to occur to him that she might want to know where he was—or maybe it did, and his not telling her was his way of saying that she didn't have the right to know.

She might be seeing things that weren't there,

but if he didn't communicate what else could she do? It made it incredibly difficult to develop a really intimate connection—but maybe that was the point. He didn't want intimacy outside the bedroom, and she—

Grace had stopped fighting the knowledge that she had fallen in love with him and had decided to simply live in the moment and deal with the inevitable pain when it arrived.

Tonight, the future did not lie heavy on her mind. Tonight it was occupied with big things, like whether to wear her hair up or down…

The decision was delayed when her mobile phone rang.

Glancing at the caller ID, she answered.

Her sister Hope got straight to the point. 'Is it true that you have been invited to the Luphia birthday bash?'

The jealous indignation in her sister's voice brought home to Grace just what a big deal it was, and sent her stomach muscles nervously fluttering all over again.

'Hardly a *bash*…it's just a meal. Salvatore left their charity a sizeable bequest in his will. I think it's a sort of thank-you,' Grace said, attempting to downplay the entire event, and mostly her part in it.

Her sister allowed herself to be mollified, and spent the next five minutes lecturing her sister on what to wear and how to behave at such an event.

'I know,' she ended comfortingly, 'that no one is going to be looking at *you*, but slipping under the radar might be a good thing. I know how you hate these sorts of things and they'll mostly be couples there. Oh, did the gorgeous Theo get an invitation too?'

Grace smothered an inappropriate laugh before responding. 'Well, Salvatore was his father, so I'm assuming...' she said, feigning ignorance and not feeling as guilty as she suspected she should.

Their relationship was never likely to reach the public eye—it might not even reach next week, she reminded herself, thinking it was not good to build castles in the air when you were standing on quicksand. But even if things had been different she would still have kept Theo clear of her family for as long as humanly possible.

It wasn't just George who had fallen under the spell of her family—virtually every person she had ever taken home had been charmed by them. She had always been philosophical about the situation. But this was different. Theo was hers and she didn't want to share him—especially with her family.

Except, of course, he wasn't hers. But that

thought she locked away behind closed doors in her head, for study and tears at a later date.

Grace was living in the present and for once she was not planning sensibly for the future. She now knew that you couldn't plan for anything—including who you fell in love with.

George, bless him, had been right about that.

'You must see something of the man,' said Hope. 'He owns half your palazzo, or whatever it's called.'

'It's a big place.'

'Maybe I'll get to see it one day,' Hope said pointedly.

Grace gave a noncommittal grunt.

'Well, I expect some juicy gossip—so do make an effort, Grace. I can't believe you don't even know who Theo is dating. There must be some clues if you bother looking. There's a lot of speculation… He's not been seen in the usual places for a month now. Anyway, enjoy yourself,' she finished generously. 'Oh, and George sends his love…' There was a slight pause before she added drily, 'As always.'

Grace put her phone down, congratulating herself on dodging a bullet and thinking about that cryptic little *'as always'*. It took her only two seconds to dismiss the idea that her sister was jealous of her.

She felt like a coward, because her family

knew nothing about her and Theo and Grace had every intention of maintaining total radio silence on the subject. She was salving her conscience by telling herself that, realistically speaking, there was not much point, and that the likelihood of them finding out before there was nothing to tell was low to zero.

Grace tried not to focus on the 'nothing to tell' eventuality and focused on her determination to extract every last ounce of pleasure out of being Theo's lover—to store up as many memories for what she saw as a pretty bleak future for her love-life as possible.

She knew now that any future that didn't have Theo in it would be bleak. Because for better or worse she had fallen in love with him, and he was definitely a hard act to follow!

She tried to bury her feelings, terrified that he might guess. But the truth was that ever since the first time they had made love, when she had floated back down to earth and stroked his hair as he fell asleep, his head against her breasts, she had known that she was in love and that this would all end in tears.

But in the meantime she was going to enjoy it, she told her mirror image defiantly, before turning away to carefully pull up the invisible zip of the dress that fitted her as if it had been made for her—which it had.

If Hope knew, she'd be wild with jealousy.

When a team from the couturier had arrived earlier in the week Grace had been utterly gobsmacked, looking to Theo for an explanation. He hadn't seemed to think one was necessary—which was probably to be expected of a man who had never bought a suit off the peg in his life.

'You must see something of the man!'

Her sister's words came back to her as an image of the last time she had seen 'the man' slipped through Grace's head. He had been rolling out of bed when it was still dark, the golden flesh of his broad sculpted back gleaming in the half-light. She had reached out and trailed her fingers down his warm skin and he had turned his beautiful head, a blur in the dark, caught her hand and lifted her palm to his lips before apologising for waking her.

'Any time, big boy,' she had joked, in an exaggerated husky purr, and he had laughed.

Even the memory of the warm sound made her shiver.

'I need to make a few calls,' he'd told her.

She had sighed. He was on Los Angeles time at the moment—apparently there was a big merger in the pipeline there. Grace didn't know the details, but it did seem to her that it would surely have been easier for him to travel to the States rather than come to bed in the early hours, having retreated to his office after dinner and worked straight through. Or, like today, got up around one or two a.m. to conduct business.

One thing she had learnt about Theo was that he functioned on very little sleep—which from her point of view was a plus! No matter what his schedule, he did not neglect their shared bed—which was her bed. Though he never once referred to it as *their* room, even if it was littered with his belongings. Maybe because there was no 'we' in his head…only in her heart.

Oh, God, if I carry on thinking like that I'll cry and ruin my make-up.

Grace had refused to have someone come in and do it for her tonight—she had to draw the line somewhere. Though she had agreed to a lesson from a well-known make-up artist. There had barely been time for her to catch her breath after he'd left, leaving behind what felt like a lifetime's supply of designer make-up for Grace—who was a 'smudge of gloss and sweep of a mascara' sort of girl—before the designer had turned up for her second dress fitting.

They never mentioned in the stories how intensive and boring it was being Cinderella, or how much effort went into looking groomed and glossy.

Which she did, she decided now, looking into the mirror.

'Should I wear my hair loose?' she asked her reflection, her lips twisted into a grimace of indecision.

She wanted to get it right.

She wanted Theo's eyes to darken with desire when he saw her.

Her lips tugged in a secret little smile at the prospect as she walked across to her dressing table and picked up a sapphire collar necklace from its velvet bed.

Theo had said the sapphires were the same colour as her eyes. She had shivered at the touch of his fingers on her skin as he had fastened them and declared them perfect—declared *her* perfect.

The shine in her eyes had dimmed slightly when he had prosaically pointed out, in response to her protests of it being too much, that it was half hers anyway, and that it was better she wear it than it sit in a bank vault somewhere.

'There are other things you might like too,' he'd told her.

She fastened the sapphires herself now, compressing her lower lip with her pearly teeth as she struggled with the clasp. The gems felt cool against her skin as she walked back across the room to look at the results of her efforts in the mirrors that lined one wall.

The dress that had been made for her was of bias-cut black silk, deceptively simple in style. The sleeveless bodice was modest in the front, moulding her small high breasts, and fell into a dramatic low vee at the back, almost to her waist—which was why she had chosen to put her hair in an up-do, the chignon softened by the tendrils she had artfully arranged to frame her face.

The style did make her appear taller—an effect aided by the spiky pointed heels held on to her slender feet by wide, gem-encrusted cushiony velvet straps.

She knew she looked good, and knowing it was a confidence boost—not that she fooled herself that anyone was going to be looking at her with a glamorous Hollywood actress in attendance. The truth was that Grace didn't *want* to be the centre of attention—she wanted to be the centre of *Theo's* attention.

Moving restlessly across the room once more, she bent over the dressing table and applied a fresh coat of lipstick she didn't need, then promptly smudged it. She regarded her extended hand, visibly shaking, with a mixture of exasperation and dismay. Luckily the butterflies in her belly were less obvious—at least to anyone but her.

She was nervous. Not because of her famous hosts or the prestigious names on the guest list at the black-tie dinner, but because this was a first, of sorts. The irony was, of course, that she really did not know if she was attending as Theo's date or, as she had told Hope, as joint beneficiary of Salvatore's will.

It would not have been difficult to find out— she could have just opened her mouth and asked.

She closed her eyes and felt her stomach quiver—this time not with excitement or nerves but with self-disgust. When had she started avoiding asking questions when there was a chance that she wouldn't like the answer?

Sometimes she felt as if all those unvoiced questions would explode out of her—after all, what would she learn that she didn't already know? She was crazily, madly in love with Theo, and he just wanted sex.

Her mouth firmed. No, there *had* to be more. His lovemaking could not be so heart-racingly tender if he didn't feel *something* for her.

She gave a small sigh and reached for her lipstick again. This was a conversation she had had with herself a dozen times, and it had never reached a point where she'd put her optimistic theory to the test.

She redid her lipstick and walked across to the marble mantelpiece, where the gold-embossed invitation was propped behind an art deco statuette.

She was not going as an anonymous 'plus one'.

Her name was there, alongside Theo's.

It felt…official. Like the next step. They were a couple on the invitation and Theo didn't seem to object.

Of course she could just be reading too much into it. Though that morning it had been Theo who had suggested inviting her family for a visit.

'Seriously?' she'd said.

He'd searched her face. 'You don't want them here?' he'd asked.

And have you fall under their spell?

She veiled her eyes. 'Of course I do. Just maybe not yet…'

'You're afraid I will embarrass you?'

'I'm afraid *they'll* embarrass me!' she retorted.

'I will be on my best behaviour.'

She had thrown him a look of pouting challenge and affected disappointment. 'Not *too* well-behaved, I hope.'

'Seriously, though,' he'd said, his wicked grin fading as he'd put aside his empty coffee cup. 'There will be ground rules. I won't let them bully you.'

'They don't! I have never said that they bully me. I am not a *victim*.' The idea that she had come across that way had horrified her.

He'd shrugged. 'I happen to be excellent at reading between the lines. So, all right, they disrespect and ride roughshod over you. It amounts to the same unacceptable behaviour.'

Her smile had a smugness to it now, as she recalled this earlier unexpected declaration of war on her behalf. But the smile faded as her memory moved on to recall what had happened next. Its power made her feel warm—almost as if he were still inside her.

His throaty response to her saying, 'Anyone could come in!' had been a growled, 'Let them!'

Shocking. But not as shocking as the fact that she had allowed him to make love to her right there in the morning room, all the while knowing that if she'd wanted to, she could have stopped him at any moment.

Some days Grace hardly recognised herself…

The chime of the clock on the wall made her frown. Theo had reminded her to be ready for the helicopter transfer at seven before he'd vanished. It was a quarter to and where was he?

CHAPTER ELEVEN

THEO WAS IN the office—not his father's study which, even without the painful connections, was not large enough for his needs. Instead, he had kitted out a booklined room for the purpose of—

Of what? Becoming a home worker?

He pushed away the question. It was one of a few others he had been dodging for the past few weeks.

He held in his hand the envelope that contained a hard copy of the file that still lay unopened on his computer. For the past week Theo had thought about coming clean and revealing the truth to Grace. The truth that he was indirectly—actually, not so indirectly—responsible for the story leaked to the tabloids. The story responsible for her family treating her as though she was an embarrassment. The story that had been the subject only yesterday of some misogynist podcast investigation that went under the guise of 'public interest'.

He took a deep breath, and tried not to recognise the fear that swelled in him like a balloon when he imagined her reaction.

It could end everything.

The truth was overrated, he decided—and then thought fiercely, *I do not want this to be over yet.*

It would be one day, quite obviously—nothing lasted for ever.

His father's love for his wife had lasted for ever, the voice in his head reminded him. She had been his one and only love.

With a growl of frustration, he pushed the thought away. He had tonight's party to worry about, and the fact they were about to be seen together—something he had so far avoided. Grace seemed oblivious to the spin the press might put on them being perceived as a couple.

A flicker of shock moved like a wave across Theo's face as he realised that that was the way *he* thought about them.

He felt a fresh kick of guilt as he thought of Grace being fresh meat for the tabloids.

The headlines almost wrote themselves: *She jumped out of the father's bed into the son's!*

The idea sent his protective instincts into full war mode. Still, tonight he would be able to control the story to some degree. The press attending were a select few, and their access strictly limited. If they shoved microphones in the guests' faces they knew that they would never get the gig again. And at least she would be facing them under his protection.

It was only when she saw the expressive flare in his dark hooded eyes that Grace knew she had not achieved the effortlessly elegant and chic finish she had been aiming for.

That look said she had instead landed on sensual, sleek and sizzling hot.

Her earrings swung as she tossed her head, enjoying the dizzying sense of power the knowledge gave her. 'You like?'

He growled and sighed. 'You are a provocative little witch—you know that, don't you?'

'You look very beautiful too,' she offered generously.

It was an understatement. In a formal dinner suit he looked exclusive, and nothing short of heart-stoppingly spectacular.

He held out a crooked arm and after a moment she laid her hand on it, feeling the sinewed strength beneath her fingers.

'Your carriage awaits.'

He set his teeth in a smile that she knew hid his struggle to control his raging libido.

'Actually, your helicopter. The press will be there when we arrive.'

Grace hitched up her skirt as they stepped out onto the protective carpet of fake grass that had been thrown across the lawn, making a path to the helicopter. Her heels said thank you for the thought.

'I know…you said.'

'You know that it is unlikely anyone will ask you any questions?'

'But if they do I won't say anything. I'll be fine, Theo,' she said soothingly. She couldn't really blame him for worrying that she would put her foot in it and embarrass him.

'That damned story,' he gritted. 'I am so sorry.'

Grace was touched, but gave a philosophical shrug. 'It's not your fault,' she said, and saw something flash in his eyes before he looked away.

At the other end of their transfer, where they parked up alongside three other helicopters, there was eco matting to protect her heels, and they were greeted by a uniformed team of concierges to guide them to the illuminated Palladian villa.

It was a massive edifice. The columns and steps leading up to a wide central entrance were guarded by what appeared to be statues of gods which were interspersed with ornamental fountains.

They came to a halt as a couple up ahead paused at the base of the villa steps to pose for photographs. She was aware of the pressure of Theo's hand in the small of her back, making its presence felt.

'This is pretty wow...' she said.

If she had not spent the last few months of her life living at the palazzo Grace would have found her surroundings utterly overwhelming, but instead she was able to look around curiously.

'Are you all right?' he said from behind clenched teeth when it was their turn to pose.

Grace nodded, and glanced up at the tall, handsome man beside her, thinking it was more than could be said for her escort. She hadn't realised how much Theo disliked the press till now. Despite his fixed smile, his black eyes sent laser rays of loathing at the faces behind the cameras. It was a surprise to her that they didn't all immediately shrivel up and die, so great was the venom in his stare.

She felt some of the tension leave him as they moved ahead towards their hosts, who were waiting to greet them.

Grace had seen Sophia Halton on the screen, of course, but the flesh-and-blood version was even more stunning. Topping six feet even without the four-inch heels she was wearing, the woman was wrapped in a beaded gold gown that clung to her voluptuous curves. She was breathtaking.

'Theo!' Her smile as she stepped forward, hands outstretched to Theo, oozed warmth. 'And this must be Grace…oh, you are so lovely.'

Bemused, Grace knew her smile was a little dazed. It was weird to be told you were lovely by a glowing goddess.

'So happy you could join us…' said Luca Ferrara.

With his neatly trimmed greying beard, he was a good couple of inches shorter than his statuesque wife. He appeared more restrained, but Grace liked the ironic twinkle in his eyes that suggested he had seen the effect his wife had on unsuspecting onlookers many a time before and he still got a kick out of it.

He opened his mouth, but Grace never got to hear what he was about to say as a figure in uniform, with a tray in one hand and a phone in the other, emerged to their right from behind one of the statues.

'So, Grace… You enjoy a Ranieri—?'

He didn't get any farther, and the slimy smile soon slid off his face. One minute he was standing there…the next he was up against one of the columns with Theo's hand on his collar. There was an expression on his face that she had never seen before. His features were contorted into a primitive mask of fury.

'Theo… Theo! *Theo*…' Luca's voice, low and calm, finally appeared to penetrate. 'Let the guy breathe…just a little.'

Theo relaxed his grip enough for the man to open his mouth. 'Do not say a word,' he told him.

The guy closed his mouth, and Grace heard the sound of his phone being thrown on the floor and shattering before she found herself smoothly ushered into a side room by her hostess.

'Are you all right?' asked Sophia.

Grace shook her head woodenly, aware that her legs were shaking.

A moment later Theo and Luca joined them. They were talking in Italian—well, Theo was talking—and the way he spat out his words suggested he had not calmed down yet.

'No harm done,' Sophia said with a shimmering golden calm as she ignored Theo's snort. 'Drink up,' she advised Grace, who now looked at the glass of champagne in her hand, having no knowledge as to how it had actually got there.

She saw that Theo was holding a glass of

something amber, and Luca was talking to him in low tones.

A moment later he patted Theo's shoulder and turned to Grace. 'We are so sorry that that happened, Grace.'

She shook her head. 'It's not your fault,' she said embarrassed about all the fuss. It was not the intruding reporter who had spooked her—it was Theo's reaction to him.

'Theo might not agree,' Luca said, glancing at his friend.

'We have to get back to meet and greet,' Sophia said apologetically as she grabbed her husband's arm. 'When you two are ready take the secret staircase.'

She moved a book in one of the bookshelves that lined the room and a door swung open, revealing a lit staircase.

'I'm sorry,' Theo said, when the room had emptied.

'I wasn't going to say anything to him. You know I'm not stupid. I wouldn't have embarrassed you,' said Grace earnestly.

'Embarrassed me?' he echoed. 'I wasn't embarrassed. I just…' He paused and shook his head, as if not only had he not protected her, but he was also the cause of the harassment.

She looked at him feeling frustration at his silence, his seeming distance from her. He remained closed off, while she was laying her soul out for him.

He put down his untouched glass. 'I might have overreacted slightly.'

She compressed her lips over the words, *You think?* This really was not a moment for irony.

'You've had a bad day?' she asked.

'I've had a bad *month*!' he exploded, and Grace flinched.

She'd been in his life for a month—it was not hard to read the message there.

'Shall we go upstairs?' she asked in a frigid, controlled little voice as she glanced towards the hidden stairway.

After a moment, he nodded.

They emerged into a space that made Grace blink. The room was lit by chandeliers and lined with frescoes and a series of niches in between arched windows that were open to the warm evening air. A string quartet played softly on a dais at the far end, directly next to an area that held tables loaded with silver, crystal and flowers.

People were mingling at this end.

Grace had never seen so much glittering jewellery and over-the-top glitz in one place in her life. She unconsciously fingered the sapphires round her neck…they no longer seemed like overkill.

'Hope would love this,' she said.

'Do you love it?' he asked.

She sensed his eyes on her face, but didn't look up. 'It's a bit like the zoo…fascinating, but I wouldn't want to visit every week. Although I'm not thinking I'd prefer to see the exhibits in their own habitat, because this *is* their habitat.'

But not mine, she added silently.

'Grace, let me introduce you to someone who is dying to meet you.'

Sophia, an irresistible force if ever there was one, swooped in to carry her away. And as she smiled and looked interested, she watched through her lashes as Theo worked the room with effortless ease, not amused when she saw there were often three or four females jostling for his attention.

At the dinner table she was seated opposite Theo, too far away for her to speak to him, but she was beside Luca, who was charming and attentive.

After the meal he left her side to join Sophia at the head of the table as they made their big announcement, and there was not a dry eye in the room including Grace's. They didn't produce their babies, who were tucked up and fast asleep. They just said that they'd wanted to share their news with their friends before the rest of the world.

* * *

'You look exhausted,' Theo said to Grace when they took their seats in the helicopter at last.

'I'm OK,' she said, meeting his dark eyes with a blue-eyed stare. 'But I think we need to talk.'

This only saying the right thing to keep going as long as possible was no longer working for her. It was too exhausting. She owed it to herself to tell him how she really felt, even if the truth put an end to what they had.

He nodded. 'I agree. There are some things I need to tell you, too.'

CHAPTER TWELVE

THEO WAS SPLITTING open the envelope when his personal phone rang. He was not surprised to see the caller ID.

'How is Grace?' Luca asked.

'We're just about to share a nightcap.'

And some home truths, he didn't add.

Instead he said sincerely, 'I'm sorry if we were a distraction.'

'No one noticed—and if we're talking fault it was my security's failure. Sophia is with the girls, but she wanted me to pass on a message for Grace. If Grace wants to meet up she is always available to a friend, and if there's anyone who knows what it feels like to have lies written about her it is my Sophia, the original tall poppy.'

Theo thanked his friend and hung up, promising to pass on the message.

He tipped the contents of the envelope on the table and let them fall—his version of coming clean. The paper that lay on top caught his eye: it was a photocopy of an old newspaper report.

He scanned it and felt his gut freeze. He knew that lightning did, in fact, strike in the same place twice. But this was not lightning. This was a woman being accused of theft…of using her position for financial gain not once but twice—*what were the odds?*

And what were the odds that he wouldn't have accepted her word without question if he hadn't been…well, *obsessed* with her? A woman had never made him feel this way before—not just his hunger for her, which was insatiable, but this dangerous need to reach out to her.

A snarl of frustration left his lips, no one could be as good and fine and *perfect* as she appeared.

He took a deep breath and told himself he wasn't judging. He'd give her a chance to explain herself—he could not be any more reasonable than that.

The disclaimer didn't lessen the irrational feeling of guilt he was experiencing. For that he could blame the fact there might be a small part of him that would be relieved if the stories were true.

It would mean he didn't have to think about this being more than just sex and work out where they went from here. Words like *commitment* made him uncomfortable.

'Hello,' Grace said, walking into the room and interrupting his dark train of thought. 'What's happened? You look—'

She shook her head worriedly, scanning his face.

For several moments Theo said nothing. She took his breath away, quite literally, standing there with her skin glowing, a pearlescent sheen against the stark black of the dress.

He imagined seeing her without the dress, still in those killer heels, with only the sapphires and him against her silky skin.

He sucked in a breath and ignored the instincts that were telling him to throw her on the floor and make love to her.

'You tell me,' he said.

'No wonder you coped so well with the tabloid stuff. You've been there…done that before…' he said, watching her face as held out the incriminating clipping to her.

She looked down but didn't read it. Instead she said quietly, 'This is an article about a police report saying that a nurse stole a necklace and a pile of cash.' Her face hardened. 'This didn't just appear by magic.'

She walked over to the table and moved her hand across the pile of papers lying there before she looked back.

'None of this did. You really don't trust me,

do you, Theo? Or maybe you're just looking for a back door to escape through because you're too gutless to commit to anything. Yes, you had a tough break as a child, but so do lots of people. That doesn't make them emotional cowards! Is this is what you wanted to talk about?' she yelled, bashing the heel of her hand on the papers.

'Oh, no. I wanted to apologise.' The irony of his need to clear his conscience drew a bitter laugh from his throat. 'I felt guilty. Because the guy I asked to collate this information on you went off-piste and leaked the story.'

If she had been pale before, now she was snow-white, her eyes deep blue pools of accusing hurt as she stared up at him.

'You leaked the story to that—? *You*?'

'I did not authorise it, but, yes. Essentially, the man was working for me.'

'And you let me think—? I was so worried I'd embarrassed you! Well, you came here to confess, and funnily enough so did I. No, not to this,' she added, screwing up the clipping in her fingers and throwing it on the floor. 'I wanted to confess that I love you. I was fed up with pretending.'

Without waiting for him to react to this revelation, Grace pushed grimly on.

'The Quants—Mr Quant was a lovely man...'

His family had been too, and they had been so complimentary about her work—until a necklace and some money had gone missing. She had been accused for about five minutes—until their grandson had been blue-lighted to Accident and Emergency with an overdose, and the missing money that hadn't already gone to his dealer had been found in his flat and the necklace hidden in a teapot.

'So you know what I'm talking about?' demanded Theo. 'This happened?'

She looked at his face and read the eager condemnation there, and suddenly she went cold. It was as if her entire body had been immersed in ice water.

'Yes, there was an accusation about five years ago...my second job.' Amazingly her voice was calm and steady, despite the sensation that the walls of the room closing in on her.

'Am I permitted to know the details?'

She searched his face and felt like a total and complete idiot for allowing herself to believe that she meant anything to him beyond good sex on tap.

'What would you like? Eye witnesses who can vouch for me? Some CCTV footage of the real culprit? Or will a sworn statement signed in blood do?'

She'd heard it said that hearing was the last faculty to be lost when a person was dying... Well, it turned out that sarcasm was the last thing to go when your heart was breaking. Who knew?

She knew now. Because hers was.

She could imagine it lying in a million shards at her feet, and a lump of ice in the empty space left by the vital organ.

'You're being ridiculous—and childish,' he snapped back, feeling sweat break out on his brow as something close to panic beat a tattoo in his blood, pounding at his temples.

He only knew about neat, passionless endings to liaisons. This was not neat, and this was not passionless! And they hadn't had a liaison... They had had—or so he'd thought—a relationship! And the irony was he had wanted more.

Grace was looking at him as though he were the biggest disappointment in her life. She was looking at him as though she hated him.

'I have to tell you that this sort of reaction does not suggest someone as innocent as the driven snow,' he said.

'Thanks to you, I'm not innocent any more,' she retorted. 'Sorry, that was wrong. I don't regret sleeping with you. Just falling in love with you!' she bellowed.

'Just stop the drama and tell me what happened, and then we can go back to the way we were,' he snapped out, frustrated.

She took a deep breath and willed herself to stop shaking, unable to believe he thought it was that simple.

'The way we were?' she echoed. 'What if I don't want to go back to "the way we were"? What if I want *more*? But you can't give more, can you? Well, being your sex on tap is not my idea of a fulfilling future—it's the sort of thing you can pay for!'

'Why don't you just give me an explanation and cut the drama?'

'I could explain what happened…and you could believe me or allow yourself to be convinced. But what then?'

She would never forget that look of doubt in his eyes. The shadow of it would always be between them.

'This is rubbish!' he charged. 'You're overreacting. If I am to protect you, I need to know the facts.'

'*Protect* me?' she scorned.

She wanted to scream. *I don't want protecting. I want to be loved!*

But there could be no love without trust.

'You decided I was guilty before I even walked into this room!'

The accusation vibrated in the air between them like a silent echo. He didn't deny it. He didn't even look at her. She turned away for a moment, afraid for a split second that she was actually going to throw up, and not turning back until she had regained control.

'This will probably make you laugh, but I'd fooled myself that we might have some sort of future together. I know—a joke or what? It's not even as though I can blame my parents. They never allowed me to read any happy-ever-after stories as a kid, so there's no excuse. This is all on me.'

She moved her hands in a slashing gesture down her body, as if to emphasise her culpability.

'There is no reason that we cannot carry on as we are,' he said.

She looked at him pityingly. 'If you really think that then you are an idiot. This is about trust. It doesn't matter how much you want to rip my clothes off—and if it's any comfort I really want to rip yours off too—without trust…'

She pursed her lips and emitted a whistling sound, and with it went all the nervous energy from her body. Suddenly the fire was gone and she felt empty.

If she had managed to unfasten the clasp on her necklace and throw it at him it would have been the dramatic flourish she wanted. But she hadn't, so instead she dropped her hands and picked up a pile of the papers that were neatly folded on the table, glared at him and hissed, 'You want childish? Now, *this* is childish.'

She snarled, throwing them at him.

He stared from the trail of papers leading like a yellow brick road and ending at his feet to her face. Her fierce—no, her sad, beautiful face.

He felt he had no control over the tightness in his chest.

She gave a slightly wild laugh, letting it escape her parched throat, then turned on her heel and left the room.

She made it as far as her en suite bathroom, where she bolted the door and, shoulders pressed to the wood, slid slowly down the wall.

She sobbed for something she had never had.

She didn't know for how long.

It was a knock on the door that broke her free of her miasma of misery.

She slowly pulled herself onto her knees,

then to her feet, feeling like an old woman as she shot the latch.

Marta looked at her, and the warmth and compassion in the other woman's face made her dissolve into tears all over again.

Several minutes later she lifted her face off the other woman's shoulder and straightened her shoulders.

'Sorry about that.'

Then she told the other woman what she wanted to happen next.

Marta cautioned her to pause and think—even produced some crazy story about a weather front into the argument—but Grace smiled and closed her ears. She'd had years of practice at resisting people who were convinced they were talking sense...people who thought they knew better than her.

'I'll be fine,' she said, amused by Marta's hysterical reaction to the prospect of a little bit of rain. 'I'm British—we know about rain,' she told the woman, who was wringing her hands in anxiety as Grace remained adamant.

Exactly an hour later she and her minimal baggage were in a car—not one of the fleet of shiny, high-end expensive vehicles that sat in the garages at the palazzo, but the housekeeper's own Mini, which was much less daunting.

Grace's escape plan was split into small,

manageable sections. She would complete one and then worry about the next. The trick was not to pause too long to think about it.

She wasn't thinking—she was acting. And she wasn't looking back. Although the not looking back might be a mistake, she thought with a wince, as she put the car into reverse and narrowly missed a branch that the wind had brought down in the courtyard.

It soon became clear that Marta had not invented the weather front. It was now windy and raining—a fact that was much more obvious away from the shelter offered by the palazzo buildings. She drove through the big gates and wondered if she would ever return.

It was doubtful.

She drove past the spot where she had first seen Theo and felt the tears begin to seep from her eyes and run silently down her cheeks. How could anything feel so right and end up so wrong?

She sniffed and told herself firmly that this happening now was actually a good thing. It could have gone on for weeks with her hoping and wishing…seeing things that weren't there.

It was now raining so heavily that the windscreen wipers couldn't cope. She pressed her face as near to the screen as possible. She screwed up her eyes as she tried to see the narrow road ahead. Then quite suddenly there was no road.

She gasped and threw the steering wheel to one side. The wild movement saved the car from launching out into space, but sent it into an uncontrolled skid.

Grace closed her eyes. It didn't make much difference. The windscreen was completely covered in a thick, dark coating of muddy sludge. The car hit something—and Grace's scream was drowned out by the screech of metal.

'Yes, I will be in the office tomorrow. I want to see all the team.'

Theo ignored the knock on the door as he continued to reel off a list of instructions to his PA. He paused to listen to an interjection she made.

'I don't give a damn where he is,' he snapped. 'I expect him in the meeting tomorrow and I will want a full run of the progress made.'

The door opened and he turned. If this was Grace, come crawling back with an apology for her behaviour, he'd make her wait.

It was Marta. He took one look at her face and put the phone down.

'What's wrong?'

'Grace asked me not to tell you, and I promised I wouldn't, but I'm very worried. There's been a mud slide and—and I lent her my car. You know she is not actually the best driver, and—'

'Stop and start again from the beginning. What has Grace done?' he asked with forced calm. Marta was not a woman who panicked.

'She has left.'

'Left?' he echoed in stunned outrage.

She was not leaving—he *was*.

'In my car. And now…' Marta took a deep, shuddering breath. 'Now Marco—he has just returned from his—well, that is unimportant— he says there has been a landslide on the north road and it is blocked.'

'And Grace went that way?'

The housekeeper nodded.

Theo fought his way through a rush of icy, gut-clenching, paralysing fear that was like nothing he had ever experienced before. He walked blindly across the room and pressed both hands on the desk, leaning forward and inhaling, struggling to clear his head of the image of Grace alone, afraid, hurt. Screaming for help. Screaming for him.

He shook his head. He needed to think.

'When did she leave?'

'I think two hours ago…maybe a little more, I tried hard to dissuade her, but she—'

'Is as stubborn as a mule. I know.' He touched the older woman's shoulder. 'You tried to ring her mobile?'

She nodded. 'No answer. Oh, I should have stopped her!'

'It's not your fault.' He gave a thin, bleak smile. 'It's mine.' As he spoke, he was already moving towards the door. 'Ring me on my mobile if you have any news, and get Nic to send some men down the east road towards the river, in case she changed her mind or doubled back. Let me know if they see *anything*. I am assuming that the helicopters are grounded?'

'Oh, I didn't— I don't—'

'Well, confirm it. And let them know that when the weather breaks we'll need a search party.'

Marta nodded. 'Be careful, and please—'

Theo, halfway out through the door, turned.

'Bring her back to us. We all love her.'

Something flickered in Theo's eyes.

'I will,' he promised.

Theo arrived at the garages just as Nic was pulling up in a Land Rover. The other man climbed out and began peeling off his waterproof. He stopped when he saw Theo approaching and moved towards him, hand outstretched.

His hand fell when he saw Theo's face.

Nic stayed silent while Theo explained the situation, and when he had finished tossed Theo the keys for the four-wheel drive.

'This is the toughest car we have for that terrain. Stay in touch—and don't worry. We'll have no shortage of volunteers.'

He had barely taken two steps before Theo had pulled away in the four-wheel drive with an agonised screech of tyres.

Theo kept the accelerator floored until he reached a point where the track was virtually washed away. He weaved his own path, negotiating the worst of the craters and rocks, though not all. The four-wheel drive bumped and jolted, rocking from side to side on the worst sections.

His teeth clenched in frustration he drove on and the windscreen wipers screeched in protest—and she was in a Mini.

'Typical Grace! Damn you, woman!'

Over the next couple of miles the rain lessened, and the going was easier, and Theo made better time—until he reached the end of the trail. Literally. His heart froze as he stopped the car and surveyed the devastation. A section of the hillside had slipped, leaving a raw wound. The road ahead was completely blocked with mud, rocks and uprooted trees.

Theo reached into the back of seat where he

had flung a rucksack full of emergency supplies: basic first aid stuff, a foil survival blanket, some high-calorie energy food. The flask with a hot drink handed to him by Marta was on top, with his own addition of brandy. He fastened the straps, zipped up his waterproof and shrugged the rucksack on as he stepped out.

The wind appeared to have dropped, but the rain was relentless again—a physical assault. There was no sign of the sunny spells that had been promised to follow the storm, and no sign of a red Mini.

Had she made it through before this section had become blocked?

Theo would not—*could* not—allow himself to believe that she had not. She was too stubborn to die...too hard-headed to give up.

'Damn you... *Damn you!*' he gritted, wiping away the moisture running down his face and tasting salt.

He hadn't asked to fall in love—he hadn't *wanted* to fall in love. How many people had their lives ruined by love? How many people ended up disillusioned and bitter when they were betrayed by the person they had entrusted their life to?

For years his father had symbolised the betrayal associated with love—a betrayal which had become inevitable in Theo's head. Now he knew the truth. That his father had been a victim of love too.

The problem was that people persisted in thinking that there were winners in this race to the bottom of common sense. It was not a race he had had any intention of competing in. But the idea that Grace was out here lost…hurt… His arrogance suddenly seemed astounding, his cowardice contemptible.

He had spent the last few weeks fighting the truth, not willing to relinquish control, but wasn't that what love was? You put your future happiness and well-being—your *sanity*—into the hands of another person.

He had built his protective walls so damned high that he had become smugly confident that no one would get inside. And then there was Grace… Those walls had crumbled the first time he'd looked into her blue eyes. Trust, he thought, feeling ashamed. Her total integrity had been there in her beautiful eyes.

He had let her go without a fight because he was a coward. And now he was going to find her and let her decide his future—because without her he didn't have one.

'Grace!'

Cupping his hands over his mouth he paused every few steps and called her name, his eyes constantly searching for any sign, dreading what he might see, hoping that she was tucked up cosily in a warm, dry room somewhere, nursing a glass of wine and cursing him.

He had taken a route through the debris and come out the other side as he tried to formulate a plan for what to do next when he saw it. His heart froze. The image of the twisted metal in the valley, deposited within the mud and debris of the slide, imprinted itself on his retina—a nightmare to relive for the rest of his life.

'Oh, Grace… Grace!'

He wanted to stand there and wail, but he locked the feral cry in his throat and scanned the incline below, visualising a path, picking out potential footholds and storing the information as he prepared to climb down.

Grace had thought she was dreaming when she heard her name—and his voice.

She was hearing what she wanted to hear, she told herself, her heart thudding as she scrambled over a small mountain of rubble and branches, negotiating a fallen tree with its roots exposed by sitting astride it and swinging her legs over.

And then she saw him.

'My God, Theo! Get away from there! It's dangerous! What on earth are you doing?'

On the edge of the dizzying drop, Theo

turned, the abrupt action sending loose rubble skittering down the ravine.

Grace's eyes went wide with fear. 'Come away, you idiot! You're going to kill yourself.'

Theo did not step away. He stepped towards her.

He intended to spend the rest of his life stepping towards her.

Towards Grace.

There were any number of things that he wanted to say, but the obvious one came out of his mouth.

'You're alive!'

'Of course…'

She stopped, her eyes widening, then going from his grey face to the remnants of the car below.

'You thought…?' Remorse filled her face. 'The car got carried towards the edge.' She bit her quivering lip in an effort to steady her voice and pulled a stray twig out of her hair. 'But it got caught on a tree. I think the impetus I think must have turned us around. The car continued to slide nearer the edge, but more slowly, and I knew I had to get out. But the door was jammed,' she said.

Theo saw her eyes, dark with the memory of

that moment when she must have thought she was trapped...thought it was the end.

He swore, choking on the unshed tears that filled his throat.

'You weren't there to save me, so I had to save myself. I tried to smash the window, but couldn't. Stupidly, it didn't occur to me straight off that all I had to do was open it. Lucky I'm skinny... Although even so I had to take off my sweater and—'

'Shut up!'

It was hard to talk when you were being kissed.

He kissed her as though he'd drain her—as though she was the last drop of water in a desert. He was fierce—desperate, even—but so amazingly tender that her eyes started leaking again.

When his head lifted it took her several moments before she opened her eyes.

'I saved you. Now we're even,' she said, staring up at his beautiful face and telling herself not to read too much into a kiss.

Although that was one kiss it was very hard not to read a lot into...

A laugh was dragged from his throat, which was raw from yelling her name. His eyes darkened with the memory of those last minutes, the like of which he never wanted to live again.

He would never, he decided, let her out of his sight again.

In the act of brushing mud from her wet cheek, he paused.

'*You* saved *me*?'

He left that for later and ran his hands, palm flat, down her body.

'You're not hurt anywhere…?'

'I'm fine. Just cold and—' She looked at her coated hands and grimaced. 'A bit dirty.'

His hands slid to her shoulders, then moved down her body as though he was convincing himself that she was really there, that everything was where it should be. It was at that point that he took in what she was wearing—or not. Because she stood there shivering, her shoulders hunched in a pitiable attempt to retain some heat, in a sleeveless white vest that sagged under the weight of rainwater. Her engorged nipples were pressing hard against the almost transparent fabric.

'Why are you wearing a vest?'

'I t-told you—I couldn't fit through the window with my sweater on,' she said, continuing to shake with a combination of cold and shock.

Cursing, Theo shrugged off his backpack and unzipped his waterproof, draping it around her shoulders and pulling the zip up firmly to her chin.

She looked up at him from under the hood. 'You'll get wet.'

'I'll live,' he said drily as he located the foil thermal sheet and shook it out, adding the additional layer.

'I must look ridiculous… I was wearing haute couture two hours ago.'

She swallowed down what sounded like a bubble of hysteria and he saw her try to control the chattering of her teeth.

He shrugged on the backpack and turned to her, his expression fierce. 'You looked stunning…but now you look *beautiful*,' he ground out rawly. 'And you look *alive*. I thought—' His voice broke.

Grace watched as he fought to regain control, his chest heaving with the effort.

'You thought I'd gone over? Oh, Theo, I am so, so sorry to put you through that.' Another thought came to her, and her eyes popped wider. 'Oh, gosh! I do hope Marta's car is insured with me driving. I did sort of bully her a bit to let me have it…'

'That I do not doubt for one moment,' he intoned grimly. 'Come—we cannot stand here.

We need shelter and I need—' He took her arm. 'Can you walk?'

'I have been walking for—I don't know long. It felt like an age. And then,' she revealed with a bleak little laugh, 'I discovered I was back where I started. I was almost giv—'

She shook her head. She was not about to admit that, to her shame, she had almost given in to sheer despair.

'Then I heard your voice, and I thought it was a dream, because I'd been praying so hard that you would come and… Oh, Theo, I was so afraid…'

She sighed as his arms circled around her, feeling warm and safe—well, safe and a little less freezing—as he drew her into his lean body.

Then he scooped her up.

'Before you say it, I know you are quite capable of walking, but right now we need to get into some shelter—and I need to ring the palazzo so that they can call the search parties off.'

Grace, who hadn't been going to protest, was quite pleased that he thought she was that tough, and she just pressed her face into his shoulder and hung on.

A short time later he put her back on her feet. She stood there, feeling bereft, but glad they were standing on solid ground, and watched as he extracted his phone from his pocket.

'This won't take long.'

Raising his phone to his ear, he punched in a number and she heard the call picked up almost instantly.

'I have her, Nic, and she's uninjured.'

For where she stood Grace could hear shouting at the other end—more than one voice, as though the news was being shared with a crowd.

Theo grinned and held the phone away from him until the noise subsided. 'Thanks, I will. I thought we'd head—'

There was a short pause as someone—presumably Nic—spoke over Theo, who nodded while he listened. 'You read my mind. And it's still got a roof?'

Another pause gave Grace an opportunity to study his face hungrily, loving every hollow and line.

'Impressive… Thanks for that. Ring me when the chopper is free. Yes, the evacuation should definitely take priority. We will just sit tight.'

'I've been an enormous amount of trouble, haven't I?' Grace remarked guiltily.

Theo looked at her. 'You've been trouble since the moment you arrived.'

She swallowed the hurt. Though it was harsh, it was hard to dispute under the circumstances.

He approached, one hand extended. There was tension still in his face, but the haggard look had vanished and he was exuding an almost indecent amount of vitality. He took her hand in his and led her to a pathway that was only revealed when he stomped down some brambles with his boot.

She looked at his brown fingers covering hers. Only a few moments ago she had felt unable to put one foot in front of the other, but it was almost as if he had transmitted some of his energy to her, she mused, as she followed his instruction to be careful where she trod.

'Almost there,' he said, studying her as he paused to allow her to catch her breath.

She suspected that she was running on adrenalin and sheer determination.

'Most people seem to think that having you around is worth the trouble you bring,' he said.

Her eyes flickered upwards, a question in them.

'Not all?' she asked.

He shrugged. 'I can only speak for myself.'

Before she had time to react to this revelation they were moving again. She had suspected he was humouring her with the 'almost there', but he lifted an overhanging branch and suddenly there it was: a small square building, its walls clad in silvered larch wood, the roof red corrugated metal, and the window frames painted turquoise.

It looked as if it belonged in a picture book, she decided.

Inside, most surprisingly, there was no dust. The wooden floor was neatly scrubbed and brushed clean. There were no pictures on the wall, just maps marked with walking trails and posters picturing native animal and bird life. There was a cupboard, marked *Take what you need* in several languages, and an honesty box underneath.

There was also a wood-burning stove ready laid with kindling beside a basket of dry logs, two folding camp beds stood against one wall, while the opposite wall contained a built-in old-fashioned bed frame that would be cosy when the curtain that hung across it was pulled.

Theo, who seemed to be taking in their surroundings too, put the rucksack on the table that stood in the centre of the room and looked at her.

'It seems that we have several of these across the estate. Walkers and bird watchers use them for free, on a "one-night-only-and-move-on" basis. A good innovation… We could expand on this idea, I think.'

Did that mean he was staying? How was she to interpret that 'we'? Was he speaking for himself?

So many questions… Her head buzzed with them.

It was fear of the answers that kept her silent as she watched him walk to the cast-iron wood-burner, ignite the paper and close the door before he straightened up.

'It won't take long to warm up,' he said, nodding to the flames already dancing behind the glass door.

'What was this place?'

'An old hunter's cabin. Nic and I used to camp here when we were kids. I thought it might have fallen down by now—I didn't know about this initiative.'

She nodded, surprised when, instead of walking over to the two-ring hob beside a deep old-fashioned sink set on bricks, he walked across to the table.

'Marta,' he said, opening a flask and filling a cup. 'Me,' he added, producing a smaller flask and adding a generous amount of the amber liquid it contained into the hot drink.

'Thanks,' she said, feeling unaccountably shy as she took it from him.

She took a sip of the scalding liquid, cooled by the additional generous shot of brandy which made her blink.

'We might be here a while now they know you're safe,' he said. 'The rescue chopper is evacuating a village where the river broke its banks.'

'Is anyone hurt?'

'Not seriously, luckily. The new flood defences didn't hold, but they lessened the damage. When we were children it was a different story. A flood could take several lives. I remember news clips of people being lifted off roofs. And there was once a landslide in almost exactly the same spot as the one today that took a truck with it. The driver left a widow and two children.'

Had Theo remembered that tragedy when he was searching for her? And not just Theo but all the others who had gone out in this weather to find her?

Grace realised the enormity of what she had done…what had nearly happened…and drained her cup in one gulp.

'I'm not normally so reckless.' She recognised now that she had been.

'Define "normally" for you.'

'I was just desperate to escape.'

Theo was tempted to lift the flask to his own lips, for Dutch courage, but he wanted his wits about him to say what he needed to.

'There is no escape for me—not from you.

We were always going end up here. Your actions just speeded it up. Not here as in this cabin. Here as in this moment.'

He paused, the effort of lowering his guard almost physical, and then pushed on.

'I might have spent another week, another month, arguing with myself, debating, hating you, loving you…but I would have reached this point eventually and come running after you. I refuse to believe, Grace, that fate would have robbed us of this chance.'

Grace's breath caught as their eyes connected, and the message in his sent her heart thudding. The silver sheet fell to the floor and pooled at her feet as she took a tentative step towards him, arms outstretched like a sleepwalker, eyes wide, but wary.

'Before you say anything—' he continued, in the same driven tone.

She tipped her head vaguely in encouragement. Even if she had been going to say anything she doubted she could have—her throat was tight with a hard knot of emotion.

'Let me try and explain.' He dragged a hand across his wet hair and gave a hard laugh. 'Explain? I hardly understand myself! But I'll try. When my mother died I think I associated all emotion—love—with pain. Being lonely was my strength…it was safety. And then you exploded into my life and started walking around in my head, taking up residence there, challenging my entire belief system, making me question everything, making me…making me not lonely. I never doubted you. I doubted me,' he admitted, his voice filled with self-disgust. 'I couldn't believe that I was lucky enough to have someone like you in my life, Grace. I was waiting for it all to fall apart. I could not bear to lose you, *tesoro mio!*'

He grabbed hold of the hand extended to him and reeled her in until she stood in the shelter of his arms.

'Oh, Theo, I love you.'

He looked into her face and released her hands, but only to frame her face and look down with wondering disbelief into her beautiful glowing eyes.

He held her as though she was something precious that might break, and she felt warm, safe, and loved by the most incredible man on the planet.

'If you're leaving I will too,' he told her.

She pulled back to look into his face, amazed by his declaration. 'I'm not going anywhere. I can help manage the estate.'

He laughed then. 'I don't want a manager, Grace. I want a wife.'

Her eyes flew wide, her jaw dropped. 'Marry you?'

'Surely you don't think I will settle for anything less?' he said, the hauteur back in his voice. 'Besides, don't you think it's a good idea if I'm around to rescue you the next time you decide to dice with death.'

'I think that would be a very good idea. Not that I am going to do anything so daft. Oh, Theo, I love you so much!' she cried, throwing herself at him. 'Thank you for rescuing me!'

'You rescued *me*, *cara*. You rescued me from a barren, empty life. You gave me life when you gifted me your love—'

He suddenly broke off his loving contemplation of her features and lifted his head, an expression of disgust etched on his handsome face.

'What's wrong?' she asked.

'Unless I'm mistaken, we're about to be *rescued*,' he said raising his voice above the whirr of helicopter blades low above their heads. 'Talk about bad timing!'

She laughed. 'Oh, I think it's a good thing to get back. We have another hundred rooms at least to tick off our list.'

He gave her a loving smile that melted her bones.

'I like the way you think. In fact I like everything about you—except your tendency to rush headlong into danger.'

Stretching up on her tiptoes to plant a long, lingering kiss on his mouth, before lowering herself back to terra firma, she flashed him a serious look.

'Now I can rush headlong into you, I think I'll be safe,' she said, and smiled confidently.

EPILOGUE

GRACE WALKED INTO her wardrobe and stopped.

Beside her, Marta said nothing.

'What the—? What has happened? Where are my—?'

She went to the shelf where her most used items were kept. It was empty. She looked around in bewilderment—nothing was where she usually put it. Her clothes had not vanished, but they were hung in neat, colour-co-ordinated rows marked *Summer*, *Winter, Autumn*...

Marta cleared her throat. 'Apparently the person your sister brought with her thinks you are not a spring person, and also that your shoes are out of balance with the natural world— something to do with the way they were facing. I put them in the bedroom closet. I will return them when the guests have left.'

Grace let out a little scream of sheer frustra- tion. 'I will kill her—I really will.'

'It seemed simpler not to argue. Everything

can be put back,' Marta pointed out placidly. 'And your sister was enjoying herself.'

Grace's ready sense of humour reasserted itself and she began to laugh—until Marta pointed out that she would need her make-up done again.

'Hope had her first internship at an office in a law firm,' she told Marta. 'Her second day the clerk was out of the office and she rearranged the entire filing system. Luckily it was all backed up. She really couldn't understand why people were so upset, because—'

'Her system was much more efficient?'

Grace spun around to see Theo. 'You shouldn't be here. It's bad luck to see the bride's dress before the wedding.'

'You're not wearing your dress—unless that delightful little number is what you intend to walk down the aisle in. I have no objections, but I'm thinking of the heart attack risk. There are several guests who might well need medical attention. Garters and stockings…now, why don't women wear them more often?'

'Because they are so damned uncomfortable, maybe?' she suggested, deciding that she might bring them out on special occasions if Theo liked them so much. 'You really shouldn't be here Theo,' she added in a softer voice. And then, realising that her husband-to-be was wearing jeans and tee shirt, she let out a small shriek. 'You're not dressed!'

'Neither are you,' he pointed out.

Her chest, which was squeezed into a corset, swelled. 'I have endured two hours of being primped and polished. There's been an army of people in here. We've only just got rid of them—haven't we, Marta?' She looked around. 'Where is Marta?'

'Marta tactfully withdrew to give us a private moment.'

'We'll have a lifetime of private moments. Oh, Theo, you do want this, don't you? You're not having second thoughts?'

He held her gaze steadily. 'Never,' he said simply. 'For me this is just a formality. I committed myself to you months ago.'

She nodded, loving him. 'I feel that way too,' she said huskily. 'Why has it taken so long to organise our wedding?'

'Because we have tried to please too many people.'

She sighed. 'You mean me? I know. It's just—'

'You can allow people this day and then we will have the life that suits me—' He broke off as there was a tap on the door.

'If that's my mother or my sister, tell them I'm dead.'

'Relax…it won't be. They're trying to sober up your brother, using some quite brutal methods.'

'Oh, God, which one? No, don't tell me!' she added, shaking her head as she walked past him to the door.

Her shoulders relaxed when she saw Sophia standing there. In the past months she and Grace had grown close, and last month Grace had become godmother to one of Sophia's twin daughters.

'Do you want me to go away?' Sophia said, glancing humorously at Theo.

'I have already been given my marching orders,' Theo said, brushing past the two women. 'Lovely as always, Sophia,' he called, turning in the doorway and bowing to both women.

'I don't know how he can be so relaxed,' said Grace. 'I'm a bag of nerves.'

'It's a front. Luca was a wreck. I just came to say don't forget to enjoy yourself. I'll leave you…'

'No, Sophia, don't go. They'll all be back soon, and it will be bedlam. Do you mind helping me get into my dress before they descend?'

'Of course.'

At least her sister had not rearranged her wedding dress. It was still hung in layers of tissue inside a polythene bag emblazoned with the name of the couturier who had designed it.

'Right…careful with your hair—we don't want to… Perfect,' Sophia said as Grace held her arms out. 'And let's not get make-up on the fabric… Oh, yes, that is gorgeous,' she said, admiring the silk column with its sheer lace overlay and the floating train of exquisitely embroidered satin with delicately frayed edges. 'Very vintage.'

'My grandmother wore a dress very similar, but when we got it out the moths had been at it. The designer tried to recreate it with some modern twists.'

Grace stood impassive as her friend arranged the folds of fabric and fastened the tiny silk-covered buttons in their loops, then rearranged the embroidered train and stood back.

'Oh, my, Grace… You look just— There are going to be a lot of tears when you walk down that aisle,' she predicted, kissing Grace's cheek. 'Are you wearing a veil? No, don't tell me! Let it be a surprise. See you in there, girl.'

As Grace paused outside the door her tearful sister, who was her maid of honour, took her arm.

'You're beautiful, Grace…just so beautiful. You're going knock him out.' Then, rather to her surprise, her sister echoed Sophia. 'Don't forget to enjoy it. I was so terrified that I don't remember my wedding day at all.'

Impulsively Grace kissed her sister, who squealed.

'You'll crush your flowers! Trust you to choose wildflowers… They are beautiful, though—everything is.'

Originally the service had been going to take place in the small chapel on the estate, but when the guest list had grown it had been decided to use the ballroom.

As the music started and she stepped inside, Grace was bombarded with a myriad of sensations: the scent of the flowers that filled the room, the sight of all the heads turned her way… She felt a moment's panic, and then relaxed her face into a smile as she met the eyes of the man who was already her husband in her heart.

She began to walk towards him, her steps quickening as she processed through the room. Halfway there she suddenly started to run, not afraid of falling because she knew he would catch her.

There were a few gasps, and then ripples of laughter, and then, when she reached Theo, several piercing whistles, a lot of foot-stamping and a deafening clapping as people got to their feet, the order of service forgotten in the joy of the moment.

Theo caught his bride's hand, his eyes glowing. 'Wow, you look like an angel! And, future wife of mine, do you know how to make an entrance!'

The priest cleared his throat. 'If we're ready?'

'Thank you, Father. Yes, I'm ready for the rest of my life with this incredible woman.'

When the congregation had subsided into their seats the priest began—and so did the rest of Grace's life.

* * * * *

If Awakened in Her Enemy's Palazzo
*left you wanting more, then why not
get lost in these other stories
by Kim Lawrence?*

The Italian's Bride on Paper
Innocent in the Sicilian's Palazzo
Claimed by Her Greek Boss
The Prince's Forbidden Cinderella
Her Forbidden Awakening in Greece

Available now!